P9-CQH-810

Kids' Letters to HARRY POTTER

FROM AROUND THE WORLD

Kids' Letters to HARRY POTTER

FROM AROUND THE WORLD

AN UNAUTHORIZED COLLECTION

Compiled by

BILL ADLER

CARROLL & GRAF PUBLISHERS, INC.
NEW YORK

First Carroll & Graf edition 2001

Carroll & Graf Publishers, Inc.
A Division of Avalon Publishing Group
161 William Street
New York, NY 10038

Library of Congress Cataloging-in-Publication Data is available.
ISBN: 0-7867-0890-5

Manufactured in the United States of America

Acknowledgments

I want to thank the many booksellers around the world who helped get the word out about *Kids' Letters to Harry Potter from around the World.* These bookstores and booksellers include: Norwich Bookstore, Liza Bernard; Flying Pig Children's Books, Elizabeth Bluemle; Bear River Books, Barbara Bogart; The Book Works, Mary Burns, Suzanne Dropper; A Likely Story Children's Bookstore, Marilyn Dugan; The Enchanted Forest—Books for Children, Carolyn Frakes; Edward T. Rabbit & Co. Books for Children; Avalon Books, Stefani Kelley; Little Professor Book Center in Sheboygan, Wisconsin; Moravian Book Shop; Rainy Days Bookstore, Suzy Turcotte; White Birch Books, Donna Urey; Chinook Bookshop, Cristen Van Vleet; Great Horned Owl Children's Bookstore; Borderlands Books; The Red Balloon Bookshop; The Little Bookshop; Hobbit Hall; Hicklebee's; Butterfly Books; Books of Wonder; B. Macabee's Booksellers; The Bookery; Millrace Bookshop in the Gristmill; Baileywick Books, Inc.; Second Story Book Shop; The Bookmark; Storybook Cove; Bookends; Bookshop Santa Cruz; M is for Mystery; Jeannie Kaufman; Giant Steps, The Book House of Stuyvesant Plaza; Cody's Books, Melissa Mytinger; Accent On Books; The Book Depot, Larry Baker; Summer Street Books, Larry Proulx; Broadside Bookshop; Booksmith, Bob Hegarty; Lowry's Books, Tom Lowry; Saturn Booksellers, Jill Miner; The Book Shop; Read All About It Bookstore; Reading on Walden Bookstore; Anderson's Book Shop; Women Children First; Books on Vernon; Alibi Books; The Sly Fox; Sandmeyer's Bookstore; The Bookstall At Chestnut; Court Bookstore; Kids Ink; Danner's Books, Susan Danner; The Book Depot; Enchanted Forest Books; The Book Barn; JacRabbit Hollow Unique Books; The Last

Chapter; Hawley-Cooke Booksellers; Beaucoup Books Maine Coast Book Shop; The Kennebunk Book Port; Junior Editions; Greetings & Readings; Tatnuck Booksellers & Sons; Mundi International; Booksmith; Toad Hall Bookstore; Eight Cousins Books, Carol Chittenden, Amanda Bock; Coffee and Friends; McLean & Eakin Booksellers; Horizon Books, Michelle Kelly; Island Bookstore; The Book Nook; Anderson's Bookshop; The Sly Fox, George Rishel; Hawley-Cooke Booksellers, Melissa Bernstrom; Northern Lights Books and Gifts, Laura Jensen; Fishing with Your Mind, Beth Plattner; Junior Editions Children's Bookshop, Liz Shaffer; Wild Rumpus—Red Balloon Bookshop; Fishing with Your Mind; Square Books; Columbia Books; Fact & Fiction; Chapter One Bookstore; White Birch Books; The Dartmouth Bookstore; Bennett Books; Annie's Book Stop; Bound to Read; Bank Street Bookstore; Oblong Books & Music; Mysteries on Main, Street; Merritt Books; Blackwood & Brouwer, Booksellers Ltd.; Wild Rumpus, Collette Morgan; Old Harbor Books, Don Muller; Sou'Western Bookshop; Happy Booker; The Golden Notebook; Quail Ride Books; Not Just For Kids Bookstore; Hemingway's Books & Gifts; Mantoe Booksellers; Sloan's Book Shop; Island Bookstore; Bristol Books, Inc.; The Country Bookshop; Zandbroz Variety; K&M Books; Books of Aurora, Inc.; The Reader's Choice; Readmore Bookstore; Odyssey Learning Center and Books, Inc.; Little Professor Book Center; Joseph-Beth Booksellers; The Bookseller; Annie Blooms Books; Paulina Springs Book Co.; A Children's Place; Mother Kali's Books; Outback Children's Bookstore; Mindventures; Winter River Books; Green Gables Bookstore; The Tudor Book Shop and Café; Poor Richard's Booksellers; The Bookstore; Chapter Two Bookstore; The Curiosity Shop; Davis-Kidd Booksellers; The Twig Book Shop; The Red Balloon; Baytime Books for Children; Children's Books Express; Enchanted Forest Books for Children; Front Street Books; The Read Leaf; The King's English; Walton Books; BYU Bookstore; Flying Pig Children's & Adults'

Books; The Book Rack & Children's Pages; Northshire Bookstore; Norwith Bookstore; Bear Pond Books of Montpelier; Briggs Carriage Bookstore; Deerleap Books; Likely Story Children's Bookstore; Edward T. Rabbit & Co. Books for Children; The Corner Shelf; Secret Garden Bookshop; Village Books in Historic Fairhaven; Liberty Bay Books, Suzanne Droppert; Queen Anne Avenue Books; Mostly Books; The Bookworks; Island Books, Etc.; University Book Store; Children's Corner Bookshop; Eagle Harbor Book Company; Stillwell Book Shop; Velveteen Rabbit Bookshop; Butterfly Books and Literacy Center; Little Professor Bookshop (Sheboygan); Harry W. Schwartz Bookshop; Little Professor Book Center (Oshkosh); Dragonwings Bookstore; Harry W. Schwartz Bookshop (Mequon); Harry W. Schwartz Bookshop; Bear River Books; R-D Pharmacy & Books Horizon #39; Two Ocean Books; and the Moravian Book Shop.

A special thanks goes to the Cub Scouts in the United States, England, Australia, Ireland, Japan, Malaysia, Holland, Canada, and Trinidad and Tobago, and Japan; Brownies and Girl Scouts; Booster Magazine; Clémentine Bagieu; Joram van Kempen; Katherine Slemmer; and the Girl Scouts.

Richard Robin provided invaluable translation assistance. Eleanor Young bravely typed her son's letter, as did many parents. To all the typing parents, we say "Thanks!"

As with any book, there are some people who just know how to really help. So I want to save the best thanks for last: Tracy Quinn, Peggy Robin, Bill Adler, Jr., Pat Ettrick, and Katherine Slemmer.

SYRENA DONÉ

Introduction

Nothing has rocked the children's book world like Harry Potter. Harry Potter is a phenomena that has inspired in ways that nobody could have imagined. Harry Potter has created an entire world of adventure for children (and more than a few adults, too!) Harry Potter is a world within a world: It is a place where wizardry and magic permeate things, but it is also part of our world—the place of Muggles.

While compiling *Kids' Letters to Harry Potter from around the World*, I found that not only was there tremendous interest in J. K. Rowling's stories, but that Harry Potter has inspired children to read more than ever before. I had the wonderful opportunity to talk with many children and interview them for *Kids' Letters to Harry Potter from around the World,* and almost universally, I was told that reading the Harry Potter books has whetted the appetites of these young readers. What Harry Potter has done is to help create a new generation of readers who will treasure reading for the rest of their lives. And who knows, perhaps among the children whose letters are in this book is the next J. K. Rowling!

Children from around the world wrote letters. In *Kids' Letters to Harry Potter from around the World* are young Potter fans from the United States, England, the Philippines, South Africa, Singapore, Australia, Estonia, Netherlands—from every continent.

I think that as you read these letters you will discover the force of children's curiosity and imagination. Among my own favorite letters are those suggesting new spells and potions—spells and potions I don't want my grandchildren to try around their houses.

But you didn't buy this book to read what I have to say, so I'm going to cut myself short. Without any further ado, here are *Kids' Letters to Harry Potter from around the World.*

Bill Adler
New York City
August 2001

Editor's Note

Kids from all over the world sent us letters. Some came via email, some by conventional mail. Some were collected by teachers and librarians and sent to us in a bundle. Many children included their age but quite a few did not. When the child gave his or her age we included it. We respect the privacy of those other children who didn't tell us how old they are. Also, for the sake of privacy, we have included only the first names of the children whose letters are in *Kids' Letters to Harry Potter from around the World*. In addition to their letters, many children were also interviewed for this book—those interviews appear right after the child's letter. Every child who has a letter in this book receives a free copy of *Kids' Letters to Harry Potter from around the World*.

SYRENA DONÉ

Dear Harry,

My Muggle name is Ann, but in the wizarding world, my name is Arabella Arithmancy. I am an American 12-year-old. I am Muggle-born, like Hermione. In fact, I'm a lot like her. I am at the top of my classes, I dislike "fads" and the "popular" or "boy-crazy" girls, and I'm often misunderstood, even by those close to me.

I was wondering: In your third year, you caught the animagus and you threatened to kill him if he transformed, but why didn't you just put him under the Full-Body Bind? If it wears off, you could have renewed it, and even if a strong wizard could break it, your adversary isn't exactly a strong wizard.

Anyway, thank you for bothering to read this.

Sincerely,
A. Arithmancy
Chula Vista, California
Age 12

Interview with Ann

Ann has long been a self-described "fantasy freak," but for her the Harry Potter books were not just another magic-wands-and-wizards series. In her words, "Until I read the Harry Potter books, it was only reading. I read fantasy, that was it. After reading the books, though, I turned into an author—a writer, I imagine. Now I scrutinize and analyze books. . . . It's a different way of looking at things, and it has made me better appreciate what authors do and the works they create. I can now reread books and appreciate their value in sparking children's imaginations all the more.

I asked her what she liked best about the main character. Ann explained, "The thing I like most about Harry Potter is that he's not perfect, and that he relies on friends for a lot. Friendship is a heavily stressed value in the books, and I love how it makes me feel when I think about what he has to face, and then I think about who he has to face it with."

"Do you have any other favorite characters?" I asked her next, "and why?"

"My second favorite character," Ann replied without hesitation, "is Hermione Granger, because she reminds me of me. We have the same kind of personality—academic, but working on loosening up and making friends."

Since she'd told me her own reasons for loving the books, I next wondered if she had any ideas why the series has been such a hit with kids all around the world. Ann said, "I think children like *Harry Potter* because the books have just the right mixture of mystery, magic, and unexpected plot twists. The underlying values leave a mark in them, too, and they keep coming back."

"If you could have any of Harry's powers, which would it be?" I asked Ann, "and why?" She took her time with this one, clearly wanting to pick the best one. "A power of Harry's . . . hmm . . . Probably, I would find flying on a broomstick to be the one I would enjoy the most. I love the sky, and whipping through it on a broomstick sounds exciting."

"And what about a spell from the books? Is there one you wish you could use in your own life?"

Ann had no trouble coming up with an answer to that one. "I would have to pick the Cheering Charm. I need it sometimes, and it would be so much fun to go around casting it on everyone."

"Suppose you could talk to J. K. Rowling right now? Would you have any suggestions or ideas that you'd like her to use in future *Harry Potter* books?" To get her thinking, I tossed out a few possibilities of my own: "Should Harry Potter's friendship with Hermione turn romantic? Or should he try a year as an exchange student in an American school of witchcraft and wizardry? What do you think?"

Ann wasn't crazy about the first of my proposed plot developments: "I cannot see Hermione and Harry together. Hermione and Ron, but not Harry." But she liked the second scenario. "I think it would be great if the 'Dream Team' went to an exchange school! Yet another way for Voldemort to get at Harry, though. I think the only thing the books really need is for Neville to suddenly show spunk in a tight spot and save everyone. Neville needs to have a situation like that."

Are you listening, Ms. Rowling? Because poor Neville has very few such loyal fans, I suspect!

Dear Harry,

You are so lucky you can ride a broom. It sounds so fun! If I were you I'd ride a lot. How does it feel to be able to use magic? Do you think it is a privilege?

The tournament you were in sounds exciting. I liked the first task of the tournament the most.

Also, Harry, we have raccoons in our house. Will you do me a favor and cast a spell to get rid of them?

I've never heard of anybody before with a pet owl. It must be cool! Hogwarts seems like a really neat school! (Too bad I can't go to it.) What is your favorite subject at Hogwarts? I think mine might be the Defense of the Dark Arts. It seems your life is full of adventure.

Sincerely,
Karen
Age 10
Washington, D.C.

Interview with Karen

"I like Harry Potter because I like fantasy and magical things, and because it's interesting and has lots of action." So says one of the many children around the world who eagerly lined up at 11:00 P.M. (way past their bedtime) to get the fourth Harry Potter book as soon as it was available.

Like many of her peers, Karen finds so many of Harry's qualities admirable. Karen says, "Harry Potter is a nice person, and he's curious, creative, and smart. For example, he helps his friends." But what Karen likes most about Harry is his magical skills. Karen's a bit envious, too, admitting that she would like to "fly on a broomstick because I've always wanted to fly in the air, not just on an airplane. I've wanted to fly where I could steer."

Who do you think Harry Potter will marry? "I'm not sure, but maybe Hermione because they've been friends for a while," Karen says.

Hogwarts is an adventure, an incredible, wonderful place that mixes the magic with the mundane. I asked Karen, "What's better about Hogwarts than your school?" She replied, "You get to learn how to do magic." What's better than that? But Hogwarts has one not-so-great thing: Professor Snape. Karen told me, "I might be afraid of Snape a little bit because he's not very nice. He's kind of mean to people he doesn't like. I'd try to stay away from him."

Is there anything in the Harry Potter books that's scary? "They're not too scary," according to Karen. In fact, "sometimes I don't want to stop reading because the endings of some of the chapters kind of make you want to keep going."

The Harry Potter series has inspired a lot of children to read more, so I asked Karen what other books she would recommend to somebody who likes *Harry Potter.* She listed a few:

All the books by Edward Eager
Ella Enchanted by Gail Carson Levine
Voyage of the Basset series by James C. Christensen
Magic Elizabeth by Norma Kassirer
Enchanted Forest Chronicles by Patricia C. Wrede
The Phantom Tollbooth by Norton Juster
The Last of the Really Great Whangdoodles by Julie Andrews Edwards

Dear Harry,

How is Hogwarts? I hope Malfoy isn't cracking your sanity. Is Neville Longbottom melting fewer cauldrons? Are you managing to annoy Dudley enough? Maybe you can cast a spell that will make him recite expressive poetry (Roses are red, violets are blue. . . . Is Snape going easier on you?

How are Dobby and Winky doing? (My request is that you give them each a new pair of socks, or else!) The spell to make Dudley recite poetry is:

> Annoying, pesky little brat,
> A child who is way too fat,
> Recite poetry by Poe or Twain,
> Do it now before you destroy my brain!

You might want to try that on Aunt Petunia or Uncle Vernon. Is your Firebolt functioning well?

I'm afraid I can't send this by owl, but I hope you will make an exception.

Sincerely,
Rachel (Master Quidditch player
and expert enchantress)
Age 9
Fairfax, Virginia

Interview with Rachel

Has reading Harry Potter *made you enjoy reading even more? Why?*
I have always loved to read, but Harry Potter takes you into his world and all the fascinating things in it.

What do you like most about Harry Potter?
I like Diagon Alley; it's just bursting with magic. (I also like Hogsmeade!)

After Harry, who is your second (or third) favorite character? Why?
Hagrid is definitely my second favorite. I love how he raises magical creatures. He's just so nice.

If you could have any of Harry's powers, which would it be? Why?
I would want the Invisibility Cloak to sneak food to my room!

Why do you think children love reading about Harry Potter so much? What makes Harry Potter *such a wonderful book?*
I think Harry Potter is so popular because he takes you into his world, gives you tons of adventure, and overall makes you want to be there.

If you could use just one spell or magical item from Harry Potter, *what would it be?*
Oh, that's easy, his Firebolt! Geez, that would be a lot cooler than my Razor scooter.

Do you have any advice for J. K. Rowling about future books? Should Harry Potter's friendship with Hermione turn romantic? Or should he try a year as an exchange student in an American school of witchcraft and wizardry? Any ideas?
I think Hagrid should definitely get married. Other than that, no comment.

To Harry,

I'm just writing to say that I've been missing you very much. You wouldn't know me, because I'm just a nobody from the lowest grade in Hufflepuff. I've been watching you closely, but I'm not a mad killer who tracks you down everywhere. (I don't work for Vol-oops, You-Know-Who.) You see, ever since the holidays began, and we all went home (apart from you), I felt very sad because I wouldn't see you again until school (Hogwarts) started again. Well it's started again, so I'm not so sad anymore.

Enough of this creepy stuff, let me tell you the other reason why I'm writing. I'm also writing because the seeker for our Hufflepuff Quidditch team is very ill, and we need a new captain, and since your team isn't playing at the moment, could we please borrow you just for practice (not for the team points thing)? Anyway, let me know by sending me an owl. My name is below.

Signed,
Michelle
Capetown, South Africa

Dear Harry,

How are the Dursleys treating you? I hope good. I think that you should cast a curse on Draco, maybe the one Mad Eye Moody used on him. It sure is creepy with Voldemort back. I am sort of afraid.

Why do you think the Sorting Hat would even think of putting you in Slytherin? Is Colin Creevey still annoying you? I feel really bad and sad about your rival dying. A question that is stuck in my mind is why does Dumbledore want you living with the Dursleys? I think you would be safer if you were with a wizard family. Like, let's say the Weasleys. Well, got to go.

From,
Kevin
Age 11
Stratford, Connecticut

P.S. Who do you think is going to win the next Quidditch World Cup?

Interview with Kevin

I asked Kevin, who lives in Connecticut, if reading *Harry Potter* has turned him into more of a reader. Here's what Kevin told me: "Yes, because J. K. Rowling opened the door for me into a new world of fantasy and fiction." What Kevin likes most about *Harry Potter* is "the idea of a wizard school and wizards living in secret." It seems that

Kevin's notion is shared by many kids—how wonderful it would be to be a wizard and be a classmate of Harry Potter's.

I asked, "After Harry, who is your second (or third) favorite character?" Kevin's answer was an emphatic Lee Jordan "because he has a strange, interesting personality like me." Kevin talked about his favorite Harry Potter powers. Here's what he said: "I would want to be a wizard so I could go to Hogwarts and see all the different, unusual things, and sports like Quidditch." His absolute favorite wizard power is "the broom." Why? "Because I also wondered what it is like to fly," Kevin said.

Kevin has a keen interest in J. K. Rowling's next Harry Potter book. Here's what he thinks: "I think J. K. Rowling should take her time writing the books. That way they are better and also because if she wrote too soon I would read them too quick and the wonderful world of Harry Potter would be over." What a sad thought—that one day there might not be any new Harry Potter books!

Dear Harry,

What's new? How are things over there at Privet Drive? I hope Dudley is on a better diet than last year so you don't have to eat old cakes that you've hidden from your aunt and uncle. Harry, I know this may sound a little silly, but I think you should learn how to perform the Avada Kedavra curse, so that in case you run into Voldemort or one of his crazy supporters, you know how to finish them off before they have the chance to finish you off. I hope you catch them soon, so you can go and live with your wizard godfather and leave the Durs-leys for good.

Good luck with school next term and be sure to say hi to Ron and Hermione for me.

From,
Donovan
British Columbia, Canada

Dear Harry,

Hi! I'm Karen from the Philippines. So you must be really wondering why all these tons of letters came. We kids have been given a chance to write to you. I really feel lucky I have been given this chance. [Had I been a year older, then I would not have had the chance.] I just turned 15 this twentieth of December.

Though our worlds are far apart (you in Britain and me in Asia), I think we have a connection. You see, we have lots in common. You are a wizard-special, great, something to be amazed at. Well, I'm also a wizard, but I don't do magic. I'm a wizard in school, and I'm good in my academics. But I'm not a nerd. I also get into mischief, and my teachers often get exasperated. Aside from that, I also have many friends. There are seven actually who are the closest to me. Like Ron and Hermione, they often get me into and out of trouble. Though we are tried and tested, we still stick close together.

Oh, I almost forgot: You and I practically have the same school. No, I don't go to a wizarding school but Philippine Science High School is almost like Hogwarts. In a way it is. It's a special school for gifted students (and I'm one of them!). We have advanced classes and technology lessons. But when much is given, much is expected. It's definitely exhausting! I often stay up late just to finish homework. And besides, we also don't have all our parents around all the time. You're an orphan already, right? I still have my both parents alive, but my father works abroad, and he comes home once a year. I really miss him terribly, especially during Christmas, and he misses me, too. But I know you miss your parents even more. Not even magic can bring them back.

Though you live in a world very foreign to me, I feel like I know you. Maybe I see myself in you. Not in magic, but I can relate to the way a growing kid manages to live through life's surprises. I still believe in magic, though. When I was a kid, I used to believe in fairies. Now that I'm older, I believe in you. It's really hard to believe things are real if you don't see them. As they say, "seeing is believing." But with you, I don't have to see spells and charms. It's you that makes magic a reality.

May you have a Merry Christmas.

Sincerely,
Karen
Age 15
Davado City, Phillipines

Interview with Karen

Has reading Harry Potter *made you enjoy reading even more? Why?* I like reading books but I hate those that are too thick and with too many flowery words. With *Harry Potter*, I was first discouraged because it was thick but when I started to read it, I was spellbound! Although the book was thick, it was okay because the words were direct to the point. I couldn't put the book down until I finished it. Before, whenever I read books, I would sometimes stop halfway because I would be too tired to read but with *Harry Potter*, I would even read it until the stroke of midnight. Yup, *Harry Potter* made me enjoy reading more. Well, I read a lot but mostly for educational and research purposes. I stopped reading fiction books when I started high school (I was 12 then). Now, I really take time to read books like *Harry Potter* because they bring back the fun in reading. I can even imagine what Hogwarts, Harry, Ron, and Hermione look like. That's what I like about books—I can create my own big-screen version of it in my mind—even if the movie of *Harry Potter* hasn't been released yet.

What do you like most about Harry Potter?

The thing I like most about Harry Potter is that . . . he's a wizard. (Duh!) Aside from that, he has other qualities that I like: For one thing, he has a mind of his own. He's still young but he knows how to take responsibility for his own decisions. He also stands up for what he believes is right. He's brave enough even though he's fighting against the grain. Another thing is that he can be very smart, and he can think with a clear head even during dangerous situations. That really makes him tough to beat. But the thing I really like most about Harry Potter is that . . . he's not perfect. I like his imperfections in a way that it can help me relate to is character. I mean, sure he's a wizard and everything but he's also a kid like any of us—someone who has problems, emotions of happiness and sadness, feelings of love and hate. And I think that makes him very magical.

After Harry, who is your second (or third) favorite character? Why?
I really don't have a second or third favorite character because after Harry, they're all equally special to me. But I took a shine on Harry's third year (if I'm not mistaken) Dark Arts Teacher Remus Lupin. I really like his character because he's not very temperamental, and he taught the students many things. He's really a good teacher. And even though he was a werewolf, he did not eat people and instead hid himself to be safe. That's what I call self-sacrifice, and I think that makes him very special. I hope he will go back to Hogwarts and be cured of being a werewolf.

If you could have any of Harry's powers, which would it be? Why?
Everything! Well, not really everything. I think talking to snakes is cool but people might stare. Conjuring spells is okay, too. But the thing that I really like the most is Harry's special abilities in Quidditch. I think his good playing skills are magical, too. The reason is that Harry's quickness, agility, and fast reaction time could help me in my sport—tae kwon do. It's a form of martial arts that would need Harry's skills. I would really want to be quick and keen in sparring so that I can score many points. Just like Harry, I have big dreams for my sport. I dream of winning tournaments, earning my blackbelt, joining the Olympics. . . . Well, dreams are dreams. I'm not really super good in tae kwon do but if I had Harry's skills then I think I might just make it to the top!

Why do you think children love reading about Harry Potter so much? What makes Harry Potter *such a wonderful book?*
I really don't know. Maybe it's just magic . . .

If you could use just one spell or magical item from Harry Potter, *what would it be?*
I think it would have to be the one Hermione used to go back in time.

I have the same problem with her—not having enough time to do everything I want!

Do you have any advice for J. K. Rowling about future books? Should Harry Potter's friendship with Hermione turn romantic? Or should he try a year as an exchange student in an American school of witchcraft and wizardry? Any ideas?
I don't think Harry and Hermione are meant for each other. I think it's cuter if Hermione and Ron end up together. In *The Goblet of Fire,* Ron was kinda jealous of Krumm, and Hermione was hurt when Ron didn't ask her to the ball. So I really think they have feelings for each other, and it would be best to develop the relationships from their petty arguments. As for Harry, maybe he and Ginny would work out. Maybe.

Dear Harry Potter,

When I am at home, my parents always seem to bug me and make unfair decisions when it comes to what my rules are. I feel that I can relate to your situation with the Dursleys. The Dursleys are frequently unreasonable. Not allowing you to do your homework, depriving you of food, and encouraging Dudley to be mean to you, is intolerable.

After thinking about our common situations, I have thought of a perfect solution. It is called The Agreeable Potion. This potion causes the victims, our guardians, to become oblivious to our faults. This will result in them not yelling at us and accepting us despite our faults.

After experimenting with many different methods and ingredients, I think I have developed a magical potion using many substances with which you are familiar.

The ingredients and directions are as follows:

Ingredients

Dried nettles
Crushed snake fangs
Powdered horn of a bicorn
Porcupine quills
Mónkshood
Horned slugs
Fluxweed

Directions

- The first and most important ingredient is the fluxweed. It must be picked at the full moon.
- The nettles will take a fortnight to dry.
- Brew all ingredients in a cauldron for six hours.
- Strain the liquid through cheesecloth, allow the liquid to collect in a small flask.
- Cool liquid overnight.
- Transfer potion to a spray bottle at the midnight hour.
- Apply potion by spraying six squirts to each victim's pillow, twenty-five minutes before they go to bed.

- Potion takes effect overnight, and lasts seventy-two hours.
- Apply again as necessary.

Finding some of the ingredients for the potion can be an adventure in itself. (Some may only be found in the depths of Snape's personal potion cabinet.)

I hope that my potion works and life for you with the Dursleys, and for me with my parents, improves. I can't wait to hear your observations and about any side effects that may occur.

Keep in touch,
Kathleen
Age 14
Washington, D.C.

Dear Harry Potter,

You are so brave. I can't imagine what must have been going through your head when you battled Voldemort during your fourth year at Hogwarts. I was so impressed when I heard about it. I was very proud of you when I learned that you didn't keep the prize money. What a noble thing to do!

I must say, I was very sorry that you couldn't go to the dance with Cho Chang. However, don't worry about it, I think she really likes you.

I hope you had a good summer break after your fourth year. You sure deserved it. Maybe you'll even get to go to the Quidditch World Cup again. Hopefully, it won't be so much of a disaster this time.

Well, I have to go to Diagon Alley to buy some more robes. Hope you have a fun year.

Sincerely,
Julie
Age 12
Cincinnati, Ohio

P.S. Say hello to Hermione, Ron, Dumbledore, and Dobby for me.

Interview with Julie

First I asked Julie how the Harry Potter series affected her love of reading. She answered: "I have always enjoyed reading. The Harry Potter books weren't what encouraged me to start reading because I already loved it. However, after reading a Harry Potter book, I get in a mood where I read lots of books. It reminds me how much I love reading."

"What specifically do you like or admire about Harry," I asked next, and she answered: "I think what I like most about Harry is how he is very brave and loves to go on adventures, but never gets a big head about it. He is always nice (except when he needs to be mean to people like Draco Malfoy). I love sitting on the edge of my seat while reading about his adventures."

"Are there any other characters you like as much or almost as much as Harry?" Julie's answer: "Next to Harry, I really like Hermione—when she's not her bossy self. She's the one who keeps everyone from nearly killing themselves by using her head first. However, she is always a great friend and always willing to go on adventures when they aren't really dangerous."

"Is there a magic power from the book that you've wished you could have?" Julie said, "I don't know if it's really a power, but it would be the Invisibility Cloak. That would be really cool. You could go all sorts of places, and no one would know. Being able to fly on broomsticks wouldn't be bad either."

Julie was clear on what she like most about the book, but I asked her why she thought other kids liked it so much. Here are her thoughts: "Every once in a while a book comes along that captivates nearly a whole country. This is one of those times. The Harry Potter books are great for all sorts of reasons. They appeal to a whole range of ages, from little kids to adults. Not many books can do that. Also, the books were written very cleverly, some of the ideas are wonderful. There is hardly a moment where you aren't sitting on the edge of your seat or laughing. You always feel what the character is feeling. It's hard to pass up books like that."

Finally, I asked if she had any advice for J. K. Rowling about future books? Should Harry Potter's friendship with Hermione turn romantic? Or should Harry try a year as an exchange student in an American school of witchcraft and wizardry? She wasn't stumped for ideas.

"I don't think he should fall in love with Hermione," Julie replied emphatically. "However, a romantic relationship with someone you wouldn't suspect would be great—even Cho Chang wouldn't be bad.

It would add a twist to the story if it was someone from Slytherin. I think the story is best when it takes place at Hogwarts. Maybe Harry could battle with Voldemort in another form. Maybe Sirius could be at risk. Although, I know it was sad, but the death in Book Four helped you realize how mean and horrible the Dark Lord was. Maybe Voldemort should come back to power and kill a few more (although no one too close to the reader!)."

Dear Harry,

I'm 12, and I'm going to get grief from my friends and classmates, but I love your adventures and mysteries. I know a lot of people who like your books, too, such as my mom, my English teacher, and oh yes, half my class.

Of course, there are some people who hate the books. But that's expected with great things. I tried out for the part of Hermione in your movie, but the casting director won't let Americans in the movie. Oh, well. I do look, act, and think like Hermione, though. Brown hair, big front teeth (I know they were altered in Book Four), and top grades.

One thing Hermione doesn't have as much of is courage. That's where you excel. I'm afraid of teeny spiders on a wall, and you faced Aragog in your second year! How did you do that? Well, I guess living with the Dursleys for most of your life gave you that courage.

About Ron, what's up with him? He's gotten so odd lately. Are you going to give him a Niffler for his birthday? You should.

He could keep it in his backyard with the lawn gnomes. By the way, why aren't Ron's or Hermione's birthdays mentioned? They should be, as they're your best friends.

Well, I just wanted to let you know, Harry, that your books are the best I've ever read. I, and all the world, am waiting for Book Number Five. I read Book Number Four in one day!

Have a good series,
Tasha
Age 12
Garden City Park, Long Island,
New York

Interview with Tasha

Has Harry Potter *changed your attitude toward reading at all?*
It's made me enjoy reading more. Some parts of Rowling's books are funny, some are exciting, and others you can just relate to. If there were no Harry Potter books, reading wouldn't be as fun for me.

What do you like most about the character?
That he's just a normal kid. Well, at least as normal as a wizard can get. He has "popularity" problems and girl trouble quite often. He also has real feelings that you wouldn't expect from a celebrity.

After Harry, who's your next favorite character?
Hermione Granger. I even tried to audition for the Harry Potter movie to be in Hermione's shoes, but alas, I am American.

If you could have any power from any of the books, what would it be?
I would want it to be either flying on the Firebolt or using the Invisibility Cloak. They aren't really "powers" but they seem like fun!

What do you think accounts for the huge success of the Harry Potter books?
I think kids love Harry so much because of the fact that they can relate to him. He is also a good "superhero" type for boys, but has that touch of fantasy for those magic lovers. Kids can look up to him because he seems so real. He isn't the top student, he's a trouble-maker (sort of), but he still has skills in sports, like many people.

What about Harry's future? Where do you think his relationship with Hermione is going? Do you think it might turn romantic?
I am really not in favor of Harry being Hermione's boyfriend. I would rather have Ron and Hermione go on a date. I think that is the direction that J. K. Rowling is heading in, and they will probably fight so much that they will break up and stay friends. I think Harry should stay with his crush, Cho Chang. At least he had the guts to ask her out once!

Dear Harry,

It's me, Erik! How's Hedwig? I hope you settled your fight with Ron! I hope you win the Triwizard Tournament this year, too! I was wondering if you could come and play Quidditch. (We could attach rockets to my mom's broom so that it can fly!) I am really sorry about your mother and father. Some-day I hope we'll meet!

Sincerely,
Erik
Age 8

Dear Harry,

What's going on in the wizarding world? Hope you're having fun. Is Hermione okay? Because she sure sounded pretty during the Yule Ball. Heh-heh.

How are you feeling after the battle with You-Know-Who? Well, I will talk to you later!

From,
Alex
Kansas City, Missouri

Dear Harry,

Quidditch is the best game ever! I wish I could be a Beater like Fred and George. I think that is the best. No offense to you, of course. The seeker has the most important job, and you are very good at it. Anyway, could you ask Hermione to please give me the list of ingredients needed to make the Polyjuice Potion? I'd really like to try it out. I could find out a lot of cool stuff about people!

I still cannot believe how things turned out at the end of your first year at Hogwarts. I never would have thought things would turn out the way they did with Snape and Quirrel and all that. The strangest thing was about Snape–it would have been nice to get rid of him! I'm sure you would have liked to get rid of him and maybe have your potions blocks free!

What is the deal with Trelawney? She is so weird! Although when she had that one prediction before you met Sirius, I was creeped out! Well I hope your next few years at Hogwarts aren't too dangerous. We can't have anything happen to the boy who defeated Voldemort. You saved us from probable death. For that I thank you.

I remain,
Yours truly,
Eva
Age 16
North Vancouver, British
Columbia

Interview with Eva

I first asked Eva to tell how she came to read the Harry Potter series.

"Before reading *Harry Potter* I already enjoyed reading. I (like many others) actually thought that Harry Potter was the author! I actually started reading them because they were being sold at the store I was working at, and my manager told me to get familiar with them so if people asked any questions about them I would be able to answer them. I enjoyed them so much that I have since reread them three times!"

Here's what she likes most about the character:

"I like that Harry Potter is really an average kid. He's extremely brave for his age, of course, but he struggles with homework just like everyone else his age. It seems to me that being a wizard makes things more complicated for people—but I would still love to be a witch!"

Like many female fans of the series, Eva's second favorite character is Hermione, because "I can totally identify with her! I stress about tests and projects and always follow the rules. There are people like us everywhere!" But she adds, "After Hermione, my next favorites are Fred and George Weasley. To me they are almost as important as Harry, Ron, or Hermione, because without them a lot of humor would be lost!"

"If you could have any of Harry's powers," I asked next, "which would it be, and why?" That was a tough one for Eva, who responded, "There is no way that I can just pick one!" But after a pause she added, "I guess it would be flying, though." (That was definitely the number one choice, I discovered!)

When I asked her what she thought made Harry Potter such a wonderful character, Eva put her finger on the combination of extraordinariness and ordinariness that Harry embodies: ". . . because he is a wizard and he can do magical things but also because he seems like a normal boy (except for the fact that he's a wizard!). People understand what he goes through, and this makes it great for every age!"

I asked for her thoughts about J. K. Rowling's special talents, and she pointed out how intricately the books function as a series. "The books are awesome because they all tie in together. Something that didn't make sense in the first book will make sense in another one.

You never, ever know what to expect! For the whole first book I was *sure* that the wrong character was after the Philosopher's stone!"

Next I asked her my own favorite question: "If you could use just one spell or magical item from *Harry Potter*, what would it be?"

That also drew the response, "Once again, there is no way that I can choose!"

But Eva had no trouble coming up with some strong advice for J. K. Rowling about the direction of the series from here. To my suggestion that perhaps the friendship between Harry and Hermione should turn romantic, she gave an emphatic no. "Harry and Hermione should stay just friends. I think that it would ruin the dynamic of their friendship for it to turn romantic." But then she offered this possibility: "Hermione and Ron, on the other hand, would be an interesting pair!"

"What about Harry's future at Hogwarts?" I tossed out next. "Maybe it would make an interesting change of pace for him to do a year abroad, say, as an exchange student at an American school of witchcraft and wizardry." That one also didn't go over well. Eva was firm that Harry should stay the whole course at Hogwarts: "He knows everyone there, and the characters there are perfect. You would not be able to re-create these characters for another school!"

Dear Harry Potter,

Hi, how are you? My name is Ariel, and I have a few questions for you: How did you feel when the snake in the zoo talked to you? I would have been terrified, I mean, an animal randomly talking to you! Also, I wanted to know, what is your goal or ambition in life? Meaning, what do you want your profession to be? You have many talents, and you are fitted for practically anything. I could see you as a Defense Against the Dark Arts teacher. You have so much experience in defending yourself against the dark arts that you seem perfect.

Thanks for reading my letter and God's speed.

Yours truly,
Ariel
Age 12
Manhattan Beach, California

Interview with Ariel

Reading *Harry Potter* has opened up a new world for me, making it easier to imagine adventures of heroes and heroines.

What I especially liked about the books was the morals that they teach.

My favorite character (after Harry) is Hermione. I like her because it shows that not all girls are ditsy, and they can succeed in our modern world.

The power I wish I had? Duh, the broomstick! It just has such a magical feel.

What makes *Harry Potter* such a wonderful book and character? I think that it is such a great book because of its great detail, and the interesting plots make it fun and easy for everyone to read.

Any ideas about changing the locale or the relationships between the characters? I think it is perfect how it is.

Dear Harry Potter

Would a Slytherin be able to pull the sword out of the Sorting Hat if he drank the Polyjuice Potion?

Love,
Cian from Ireland
Age 5

Dear Harry Potter:

Hi! My name is Kelly, and I'm 14 years old. I think you are the best wizard in the whole world! I love magic, and I wish I knew some, too! It must be soooooo neat, knowing how to do spells and being able to put curses on people. If I could put curses on people, I'd find one to make obnoxious people leave me alone. Is there such a curse?

I bet the teachers are really interesting, too. I've heard that Snape is really mean to you and all, but I think deep down, he's a really great guy, don't you think?

I also love Quidditch!! I wish they had flying broomsticks in Texas, because if they did, I'd play, too. I think the seeker must be the hardest position to play, but you know something? You do a really good job of it!

I hope that this year at Hogwarts, you have a lot of fun and keep out of trouble and don't get hurt anymore. Tell Ron and Hermione I said hi and tell Winky and Dobby to keep up the good work! (They are SO cute!)

Your friend,
Kelly
Age 14
Sugarland, Texas

Interview with Kelly

I've always loved reading. It's been one of those long-term passions that will never leave me. But the Harry Potter books really brought me ack to a fantasy world that I never knew existed. I've required a much larger vocabulary and a new taste in literature.

What I love about Harry is that he's just one of those people that you wish there were more of in the world. He's bright, optimistic, precocious, a little awkward at times, shy, but always right there on the verge of greatness. Gosh . . . I wish I had him for a boyfriend.

I couldn't say who's my second favorite character—I love them all soooo much! I really like Hermione because: One, she's a girl and two, she proves that girls are just as smart as boys—maybe even smarter. I also like Dobby and Winky, the house elves. They are so cute and with their big eyes and love of clothing (especially socks!), how could anyone resist them?!

My favorite spell is probably Wingardium Liviosa. I would love to make things move around for me and be able to make things fall or move without anyone noticing.

The main reason I think other kids share my enthusiasm is that *Harry Potter* is just such a magical and exciting book. It takes kids to a place they've never been, much less heard of! It totally lets your imagination get the better of you. Harry should be a role model for all kids, to never give up on your dreams and always reach for the highest star. No matter what obstacles you encounter or mountains you have to climb, there will always be someone who loves you waiting right there when you get back.

As for ideas for forthcoming books: J. K. Rowling is doing such a wonderful job, I wouldn't want to tell her anything! And Harry and Hermione [as a romantic couple]?? No way! Hermione and Ron make a much better couple! Harry should stay right where he is. I don't think her book would have the same appeal if Harry left Hogwarts and all his friends. His readers would miss everyone and everything they have become so familiar with, even Malfoy!

Dear Harry,

I hope you're having a splendid time at Hogwarts School of Witchcraft and Wizardry, and I also hope you didn't have such a terrible time at the Dursleys over the summer. (We all know how bad they can get.) Is the Gryffindor Quidditch House Team successful this year? If not, don't worry, you are such a prized seeker and have the best flying broom in the entire world! Do you think I can join you this year at Hogwarts? Could you teach me some magic or recommend me to the professors? I'll study hard, and I already know Lumos, the lighting spell, and Nox, the counterspell. At least you aren't going to my Muggle school, St. Lawrence Middle School. Our Spanish and science teachers aren't the best either, but at least they aren't as bad as Professor Snape. It must be grand to have such good friends like Hermione Granger and Ron Weasley. I have some nice ones as well-Laura is one of my prized friends. Hope you survive the school year-watch out for Voldemort!

Love,
Nicole (Great Seeker,
Animagus, and Head Girl)
Age 13
Santa Clara, California

Interview with Nicole

I have read all four of the books. I must have read them one hundred times each! Even though the fourth book is good, I especially enjoyed Book Three. Book Three had my favorite characters, like Remus Lupin, and in my opinion, the best plot. It really had me surprised!

Hermione is like me in looks, but Dumbledore is most like me in personality. I'm one of those people who is mysterious and a little silly at times, but like Hermione I study extra hard and (sometimes) can be annoying and bossy at times. Ron reminds me of my friend—he is good in chess and is always there for me. Harry and I do have some things in common. Harry is like me because we both stick up for people and are there to help people in need. I'm also like him because I used to be the odd one out—not knowing my place. Unlike

Harry I'm not exactly famous or a wizard. The teachers at school remind me of the Dursleys.

Oh, I wish I could do magic! If I could do magic I might be a parseltongue or a necromancer. (I haven't seen them in the series but I'd like to be one.) If I got the chance to go to Hogwarts, I'd pack right at this very moment!

I know this would never happen but I'd like to see Harry's parents come back to be with him. Besides that, [I'd like to see] maybe some more animagi and the defeat of Voldemort.

Harry Potter inspired me to actually write stories since there is a mysterious plot in the stories. The books also teach you lessons in languages (Latin, French, etc.) They also have tricky riddles that make you want to figure them out and read more. I always liked to read, but not fantasy, but *Harry Potter* made me interested in reading fantasy and novels.

Dear Harry Potter,

So how is it at the Dursleys'? I know I would hate them, too. Maybe you can ask the Weasleys if you can stay at their house for the rest of your life or maybe with Sirius. I never knew you would be in the Triwizard Tournament. Do you know who put your name in? Well, how is Hagrid? I heard he liked that other giant lady from another school. Well, I hope it works out for them. And, oh yeah, I think you and Hermione should go out (no offense).

Well I gotta go . . . See ya.
Have fun at Hogwarts.

Sincerely,
Matthew
Age 14
Ft. Kent, Maine

P.S. Send me an owl back! My owl's name is Green Bean. See ya later!

Interview with Matthew

Matthew tells me that "Everyone should read *Harry Potter* because there are lessons to be learned, and even some good reading skills that all ages could pick up." Matthew got a big reading boost from *Harry Potter*. He says, "I hadn't liked reading all that much. But since I have read the Harry Potter books, it has really influenced my reading, and I read more now than I ever have."

Matthew shares a wish in common with a lot of other children—to fly. "The thing I like most about Harry Potter is that he can fly on a broom," he says. "And that there is a secret witchery school that nobody knows about!" Ah, to have big secrets! Matthew goes on to say, "I find that so fascinating! Also, that they can do these awesome magical tricks to one another and even turn different things into something else. I think I would love to go to that school but I would probably be just like Hermione!"

But there's more to *Harry Potter* than just Harry, according to

Matthew. "My second favorite would probably have to be Ron, even though Hermione is cool. I think Ron is almost always there for Harry. At bad times Ron is there to cheer him up and make him feel good. Ron and Harry are like a computer and a mouse. One without the other doesn't work very good. I hated the time when they weren't getting along. I wanted them to get back together so fast that I started reading faster!" That's what friendship is all about.

I ask Matthew, "If you could use just one spell or magical item from *Harry Potter,* what would it be?" Matthew replies, "I think I would use Gillyweed because I would be able to go underwater and see the merpeople, and even see underwater things that I would never get to see. I would be able to swim like the fishes. It would be the best thing to do in order to do a report on the lifestyle of a fish!"

Matthew has boundless enthuiasm for *Harry Potter.* "I think that the constant events happening is what makes people just *love* the books. I also think that J. K. Rowling is one talented writer and knows how to write in order to get kids to enjoy her books tremendously!

"The thing that makes *Harry Potter* such a wonderful book is that it is all fantasy and really makes kids think and enjoy the world of make-pretend. It makes them think how it would be to be in Harry's shoes!"

But Matthew does have some suggestions for Harry's creator. "My advice to J. K. Rowling would be to keep up the *outstanding* work and to make the books the best she can, just like she is doing now! I think Harry and Hermione should go out and be with each other. I think they would be the cutest couple in the book." And just in case Harry has thoughts about going on to someplace else, here's Matthew's opinion: "He shouldn't go to another school at all. I like the school he is in now."

SYRENA
DONÉ

Dear Hermione,

How are you? I'm pretty bored.

I've finished all of my summer work and bought my supplies in Diagon Alley last week. (I saw Parvati and Padma. They say hi.)

I can't wait to get back to Hogwarts: One annoying thing about being Muggle-born is that we're cut off from everything wizarding during the summer! The *Daily Prophet* is pretty much our only connection. *Sigh.*

Speaking of the *Daily Prophet:* Did you let Rita go? You didn't mention her in your last letter, and she's not back to journalism.

I got a letter from Harry last week. He says he's okay. His aunt and uncle are pretty civil to him and he's heard from Sirius. What are you getting him for his birthday? I can't decide.

Anyway, I've got to go now. Say hi to Crookshanks for me and write back soon.

Maria
Age 14
Cork, Ireland

P.S. Congrats on being chosen for a Prefect!

Interview with Maria

Has reading Harry Potter *made you enjoy reading even more? Why?*
YESSSSSSS!!!!!!!!!!!!!!!!!!!! Because—do you have twenty years?—everything about the books is amazing, every detail is perfect. You're surprised every time you read one of the books (and in my case that's a lot of surprises). Ms. Rowling somehow includes everything that you could possibly want from a book and in a new way every time; they have an amazing storyline, they make you unbelievably jealous, you find yourself in fits of laughter at least every five minutes, it's about magic!!! Do you want me to go on?

What do you like most about Harry Potter?
Oh, why this question? I could *NEVER* decide!

After Harry, who is your second (or third) favorite character? Why?
Also a pretty impossible question! There's something to love about every single character (yes, even Snape). Hermione is someone that you want to relate to. The Weasley twins are . . . well, they're the Weasley twins! Voldemort is unbelievably cool, James Potter (yes, I know he's dead) is still an excellent character, and so are Remus Lupin and Sirius. Ron's the best friend and the person to argue with. Hedwig is . . . okay, I should stop when I get to the owls.

If you could use just one spell or magical item from Harry Potter, *what would it be?*
Argh! I really hate these unanswerable questions! Well, you said a magical item, so I'll say a wand. (I love loopholes!)

Why do you think children love reading Harry Potter *so much? What makes* Harry Potter *such a wonderful book and character?*
I think that it's the warm feeling that you have when you finish one of the books! It's really hard to explain but I think it's because Harry

grew up with the impression that he was a nobody before he was thrown into the magical community and realized that he was a household name.

Do you have any advice for J. K. Rowling about future books? Should Harry Potter's friendship with Hermoine turn romantic? Or should he try a year as an exchange student in an American school of witchcraft and wizardry? Any ideas?

No one can advise J. K. Rowling! But if you insist! It can't be a Harry/Hermione romance because Hermione and Ron are going to be a couple. I really hope that Harry doesn't go on an exchange, though.

Hey, Harry!

I know you must be going absolutely insane dealing with the Dursleys all summer, so your greatest Muggle fan (that's me!) decided to try and cheer you up. I just hope you get to the mail before the Dursleys-I can't send by owl post!

I think I should tell you that from what I've read, Hermione "likes" Ron a lot, and he feels the same way. Maybe you should convince Ron to ask her out, and then they wouldn't fight as much! Well, they probably would still fight, but at least they'd make up afterward.

You know, it would be really nice if there was a spell so my math homework would be instantly done. Do you know one a

Muggle like me could use? If you do, tell me! Please, please, please with a cherry on top!!!

Good luck catching the Snitch next year.

Yours,
Maddy
Age 13
Carmichael, California

Interview with Maddy (Madeline)

What Maddy likes most about *Harry Potter* is this: "I love how it's humorous and great for all ages—me and my parents both."

While everyone who wrote a letter in *Kids' Letters to Harry Potter from around the World* is a Harry Potter fan, not everyone thinks that Harry is the *best* character in the series. Maddy is one of those people. "Actually, my very favorite character is Ginny—she has so much going for her, and she hasn't been developed very much," Maddy said.

Maddy's favorite wizard power is Veritaserum. Why? She explains: "Nobody could ever lie to me!"

Fred and George,

I am you guys' biggest fan!!! I mean Harry is okay, but I simply love the tricks you try and pull!!! You guys know the tricks of the trade! I can pull off anything!! I love taking chances!!! I hope that you ask J. K. to pick me!

Maybe you want to know more about me, I'm 13, and my name is Nicole. I'm an A-plus student but I'm getting bored of the same old thing! I've had my practice with my little sisters though!!!

Write Soon!!! :-) (-:
Nicloe (a.k.a. Nickie)
Age 13

(See the translation on next page, if you don't read German.)

Hallo Harry Potter,

ich heiße Amelie, ich bin 12 und komme aus Zweibrücken in Deutschland. Ich wollte dir sagen, dass ich Draco Malfoy dumm finde. Bei dem Trimagischem Tunier kommen ja auch andere Schulen nach Hogworts!

Gibt es eigentlich auch eine Zauberschule in Deutschland? Im 4. Band überprüfen die Zauberer doch deinen Zauberstab, um festzustellen, ob Winky das tote Mal hervor beschworen hat! Warum konnte so nicht Sirius Blacks Unschuld bewiesen werden? Ich habe mir noch einen Zauberspruch für dich ausgedacht: "Velare" (Das heißt, um deinen Gegner herum wird es ganz nebelig!)

Viele Grüße, Amelie
Von Amelie Tscheu, 12,
Zweibrücken, Deutschland

Translation:

Hello Harry Potter,

My name is Amelie. I'm 12 years old, and I'm from Zeweibrücken, Germany. I would like to tell you that I think that Draco Malfoy is stupid. There are other schools that come in after Hogwarts at the Triwizard Tournament. Is there really a school of wizardry in Germany? In Volume Four, the wizards test out your magic wand to determine whether Winky has raised the dead. So why couldn't that prove Sirius Black's innocence?

I've come up with one more magic test for you: Velare (i.e. to surround your opponent in fog).

Best regards,
Amelie
Age 12
Zweibrücken, Germany

Dear Harry Potter,

We're Dutch Cub Scouts, and we really loved to write you a letter, so here it is!

We think you should use your Invisibility Cloak a lot more often. If we could borrow it, we'd know what to do with it! We would use it to get past our parents and get to the candy! Isn't that a great idea?

We don't know all the things you can do with your magic wand, but could it be possible for Emile to borrow it? He thinks he has magic forces, too! And the only way to know this for sure is to let him swing your magic wand around!

And it would be great if you could turn all of our mothers into frogs for a moment. We'd have so much fun with that! And can you also make Titus's father and brother not argue so often? He really dislikes it when that happens.

We think it is really neat that you have books with your name in them. Could you conjure a book called *Jesper Verheij*? He'd like to have a book named after him, too! But if this letter will be printed in one, we're sure he will be just as thrilled.

Here's a question for you: Did you ever ride a broom other than the Nimbus 2000?* What's the difference? Can you make our brooms fly, too, even if they are ordinary ones? It doesn't have to be as good as the Nimbus 2000. We'd love to have the words for that spell!

Rene made a picture of a wizard. We can't send it along with this letter, we're afraid, because it's on a wall! The wizard in the picture has freckles, a pointy chin, and long, thin hair. He wears sunglasses and a magic hat with stars. Maybe you know him? If you do, please say hello from us! He seems friendly to us!

What does the Snitch taste like? We know you had it in your mouth once. That was a cool way to catch it! Doesn't

*Editor's note: Clearly, these Dutch Cub Scouts haven't yet read about the Firebolt!

it tickle the inside of your mouth? Could they use that Snitch later on again, or did you bite on it and break it? Or maybe only the wings were broken? That could be possible, too.

We made up a great spell for you:

"Frog butt without power, now you are a coward!"

Maybe you can use it against someone. We thought it might come in handy. If you read it backwards, it will be undone. Good luck with it!

Do you want to visit us? We'd like to invite you over here. You can join us by the campfire. Maybe you can make the flames turn green! That would be cool. We'll provide the drinks and crisps, if you take care of supplying the Every Flavour Beans. We are really anxious to taste some!

Well, here's the end of our letter. We hope you'll graduate without a lot of problems, but with a lot of adventures, because we'll do just about anything to read about them!

A firm left handshake,
[Cubscouts] Scouting
Subanhara-Liemersgroup
Zevenaar, Netherlands

Dear Harry,

I do hope that everything's all right at Hogwarts. Is Snape giving you much trouble? I really hope not, because he is one of the most frustrating people to me! Everything that you or any of the Gryffindors do right, you can be sure that he'll try to undo it, and I really think people like that need to take a good, long look in the mirror and get a life!

Have you got any idea what Dudley is doing? Maybe he'll stay on his diet and instead of being fat and nasty to you, he'll simply be nasty to you. (Hey, I know it's not much of an improvement, but some is better than none, right?)

What do you think that the Dursleys will send you for Christmas this year? Perhaps they'll really get you a nice gift and give you a peppermint. At least it would be a few steps up from a toothpick or a tissue!

Anyway, how are Ron and Hermione? Good, I hope. Tell Hermione that this is a spell she should try:

Shining stars
And silver light!
All that's calm
And soft and bright!
Give me peace of mind at last,
So that I can get some rest!

That may be a good spell to calm her down, so that she can forget about schoolwork for ten minutes.

I have an excellent idea, Harry! Your Quidditch team is short one player, right? A Keeper, to be precise. Well, Ron loves Quidditch. Why don't you let him be the Keeper? I'm sure he'd be great!

Written with love,
Katie
Age 13
Chesterfield, Missouri

Interview with Katie

Harry Potter has helped me enjoy reading more because it has expanded my vocabulary, and the books have trained me to look for deeper details in stories.

I especially like the Quidditch games in the books, and also I like the many different personalities. Ron Weasley is my second favorite character (after Harry) because he is always showing true signs of friendship. I would like a friend like Ron.

If I could use one magical item, I would probably use a wand, because it would fascinate me how the spells come out of it. I would probably do spells just to see what they look like and nothing more. I would also like to ride a broomstick if I could, because flying seems so great to me.

I think that children (and adults!) love reading *Harry Potter* so much because they can understand everything he's feeling. J. K. Rowling describes emotions so perfectly. I am around Harry's age in the books and that helps me get what he's feeling. Harry is a wonderful character because of his loyalty, friendship, and bravery. People will say that they like Harry because he is like them, but I don't think that's true. They like him because he is everything that they *wish* that they could be.

As for future books: I think that J. K. R. should let her own imagination run wild and not be hindered by what we want to hear, because we'll love it anyway!! I wrote a Harry Potter story (actually, it's not done) and there's a character in it from *Maple Wand School of Sorcery* in Canada. I made up the school and character. I like the sound of the name. I don't really know if an exchange student should come from it, but I like the name.

Dear Harry,

How's it going? Nothing much here in the United States. Well, except for all this president nonsense. Oh, Harry, I wish I could be like you....

Wait a minute, no, I don't. I guess the magic and everything would nice, but I don't think I would like Voldemort on my tail. Or to lose my parents. I would like to meet Dobby and Dumbledore, but I think I'd rather have my parents and sanity. Now look at me, all this time I've been sitting here envying the great and wonderful Harry Potter with all his magic and power, but not realizing the emotional baggage that came with having that name (and scar) across your forehead. Yeah, the magic would be nice, but I would much rather be a Muggle than be Harry Potter. Well, bye, Harry.

Love,
Jennifer
Age 13
Rockford, Illinois

SYRENA
DONÉ

Interview with Jennifer

I have read all of the Harry Potter books, many times over. My personal favorite Harry Potter book is Book Three because I was so happy for Harry when he met Sirius, and the plot twists are wonderful. I believe I mostly identify with Hermione Granger because she is smart, very stubborn and a very good friend. Ron and Hermione do somewhat resemble my friends in that they can all be very wonderful people, but can, at times, become very stubborn.

I think that Harry and I do have a lot in common in that we are both teenagers growing in an unknown world and exploring new and different things about that world. I believe we are different because Harry has Voldemort on his tail and all I have on mine is homework.

I would love to have magic flowing through my veins. The trick I would most wish to be able to do would be to fly. I have always wished to touch a cloud and think it would be marvelous to be able to. I'm not sure I would be able to go to a place like Hogwarts and leave my family for that long a period of time, but it does sound enchanting.

I would love for Harry to meet his parents in full flesh form to give him a chance to hug them and get to know the parents he never had. I love Harry because he is just like every other child in this world and is so incredibly humanlike, so we all can relate to him, and I love his newly found world of magic and adventure. I have always loved reading but have never fallen in love with a book so fast as with *Harry Potter.*

Hello, Harry!

I am one of your biggest fans! I am 13 years old and live in California. I have enjoyed all four of your books and am on my toes waiting for the next one. Your books I never want to put down! My mom tells me to go to bed but I say "One more chapter! One more chapter!" and it never ends. The character I like most is Hermione. Sorry, Harry, but GIRL POWER! I would never have dreamed that such a great book would come out! I have some new ideas for your upcoming books.

First, I think you should make a new character. Her name is Holly, and she is a complete brat. She is a new girl in her fifth year. She takes a liking to Draco Malfoy. She is the perfect companion for him. She is a tall, limber girl with strawberry hair in messy pigtails. A trail of freckles would run over her nose and cheeks. She is a real problem to Harry, Ron, and Hermione.

Second, I think a new spell should be that you can have any skill you like. Like if you want to do your Herbology homework, and you have to draw, you could use this spell to make you have artistic talent. But once the spell is cast, it is permanent! So you would have to choose your skills carefully.

Third, I think there should be a new class. It is like a leadership class. That means any student of third year or higher can sign up and help decorate the school and plan special "spirit days" for all the students. These students would have to wear special uniforms also verifying that they are in the leadership class.

Well, how do you like my ideas? I hope good! Well, thank you so much for your time!

Sincerely,
Chelsea
Age 13
Pleasonton, California

Interview with Chelsea

Has reading Harry Potter *made you enjoy reading even more? Why?*
Yes. The books have so much enthusiasticness, I just never want to put them down!

What do you like most about Harry Potter?
I love the action!

After Harry, who is your second (or third) favorite character? Why?
I really like Hermione. I like her because she is the only female main character.

If you could use just one spell or magical item from Harry Potter, *what would it be?*
I would choose the Invisibility Cloak. I would love to sneak around!

OY, Harry!

I'm really a big fan of yours. I know you don't exactly enjoy being famous. But I really admire your courage. You know what? Even a cockroach can scare me out of my wits! A lot of Muggles have been reading about your amazing adventures. They even decided to make a movie based on the books!

I'm really envious that you are a wizard. I really want to have a chance to study at Hogwarts, even if it's only for a day! You seemed to hate Divination—why don't you quit it, too, just like Hermione? It makes you upset and uneasy every time Professor Trelawney predicts your future. In fact, I quite agree with Hermione, Divination is just a bunch of rubbish! I think Arithmancy is quite interesting! (I hope I don't sound like Hermione, she's a bit bossy!) I also am fascinated by Potions, because I like doing experiments, adding this and that and testing them. But I don't think I'd enjoy Potions if Professor Snape teaches it! (Snape's name sounds so much like "Snap." I think the name suits him 'cause he's always snapping at other people!) By the way, how's your crush, Cho Chang? Hee, hee! I know you are blushing! Okay, okay, let's change the subject. Never mind, I'll stop here.

But be warned, don't change your attitude after receiving all these fan mails. Fame isn't everything. Don't be like Professor Lockhart, okay?

Wish you success in defending against Voldemort! (I'm not scared of saying his name!)

Your Muggle pal,
Zhang
Age 12
Singapore

Interview with Tiffany

Whenever I start reading the Harry Potter books, whether it's for the fourth or fifth time, I still feel the magic twirling me into the world of flying broomsticks, fire-breathing dragons, bubbling potions . . . Scene after scene seems to flash across my mind, enlarging my creativity when reading his breathtaking adventures. It attracts readers of all ages, mainly because of Ms. Rowling's style of writing—lighthearted, unlike the classic novels, full of the unexpected yet well described. It's a fantasy story that happens in our time—the twenty-first century, and this somehow makes it more exciting than *Snow White* or *The Chronicles of Narnia*.

Harry Potter's spirit of fighting good over evil and the streak of daring and adventure in his heart make him a wonderful story character.

Dear Harry,

Hi, Harry! How's it going? I haven't heard from you in a while, but then again, Muggle news is kinda slow. Rita Skeeter isn't still "bugging" you, is she? I haven't found anything about you in *Witch Weekly* nor the *Daily Prophet*. I order 'em even though I'm not a witch (thank God the Muggle department at the Ministry ruled not to erase my memory!) Anywayz, like I said, I haven't heard anything about you, especially after the Triwizard Tournament. Say, how did that turn out? Strange rumors are flying around about You-Know-Who, and the champion. But they're just rumors, right?

How are Hemione and Ron? Hermione's not getting too overloaded with work (and books), I hope. And did she stop the S.P.E.W. organization? I say if house elves like their jobs, you should leave 'em alone. Is Snape still trying to get you expelled? I never did figure out the guy-his behavior is so unpredictable from year to year. What's up with him? Is he or isn't he a bad guy?

Ask Professor Flitwick to teach you the Lucky Charm. What that spell does is it makes an object you select lucky. Of course, it won't do everything for you, but luck will be on your side! It only lasts a certain time period, though. It's a really neat trick. I think it goes something like: Buona Fortuna, Buona Fortuna, Journalier. I'm not sure, though-like I said, ask Flitwick!

Well, Harry, I've gotta go. I don't even know if this is going to get to you. I can't use the usual postal service because I doubt anyone knows where Hogwarts is, so I'm using an owl I found. Can all owls deliver mail? I sure hope so! Hope this gets to you! Write back soon!

Your friend,
Grace
Age 13

P.S. How's Hedwig?

P.P.S. How's your Firebolt? And is it true you're going to be the next Quidditch captain? Good luck!

Interview with Grace

I've read all of the *Harry Potter*'s, but I'm not sure [which is the best]. It might be Book Four, *The Goblet of Fire*. I guess it's because it had the best story in my opinion, so far. It has the most complex plot (which I like), and it just appeals to me. I actually like them almost equally.

I identify with Hermione the most because I feel that we have a lot in common. For one thing, she's kind of a show-off and know-it-all type of person. I hate to admit it, but I'm like that, too. But like her, I've improved, and I try to be more modest nowadays. Harry and I don't have a lot of things in common. He has this sad past, whereas I grew up in a happy childhood. I'm not sure we have anything in common at all. I'm curious, and I like to investigate stuff, like Harry, but

I don't think I'm as brave as him, so I wouldn't take so many risks. I guess I wouldn't belong in Gryffindor.

Do I ever wish I could perform magic like Harry! Ever since I've started reading the series, I've daydreamed about that. I'd like to be able to make things appear at will, or come to me, and transform things, including turning myself into an animal. I'd love to go to a place like Hogwarts.

[As for future books] I think I'd like to see something happen to Harry, alone, where his friends can't help him and he has to figure everything out by himself—something similar to the end of Book Four. Maybe he gets expelled from Hogwarts because he was framed or something, and he has to go back to the Dursleys or run away.

I like the Harry Potter books because the stories are fresh and original. They are also very well written and complete. I mean, it's like reading a textbook about another world. It seems like it could really be real. J. K. Rowling did a good job of thinking up Harry Potter.

Hi, Harry!

My name is Mike, and I would like to write a letter for your book. I am 10.

What I think would be cool is if a professional Quidditch team came to Hogwarts. They all gawk at Harry's scar (like usual). But when they see Harry play Quidditch, they are startled at how good he is and then play a game with him [and his Gryffindor team]. But it turns out all of them were from Slytherin and are Voldemort supporters, but Harry doesn't know. As usual Hermione suspects it first and tries to tell

Harry and Ron, but they're too into the thought of having a real Quidditch team at Hogwarts, etcetera.

Well, I think it would be a good start to another adventure of Harry's.

Sincerely,
Mike
Age 10

Dear Harry,

I am a fellow student in his fifth year of school (fifth grade). I have some questions about *your* world. First of all, how on earth do you pronounce Hermione's name? *Her-my-own-nee, Her-my-Knee, Her-my-own,* or *Her-mee-own?*

Next, is there a way to end a game of Quidditch other than catching the Golden Snitch? Next, does Voldemort's name really have a silent *T?*

Anyway, next question: How many classes are there and what are they? My next question is, will the books be introducing an American character? Like, say an American family with a 10-year-old wizard moves from the United States to the United Kingdom-will this be POSSIBLE??? Next of all, is the fifth book really called *Harry Potter and the Order of the Phoenix?* Next one (will the questions ever end? You bet your life they won't!), is there any such thing as a *Instant-Answer Spell?* You could answer all the questions with that. Next question (Also the-FINALLY!-last question): Will the original span of seven books really end at the last year at Hogwarts? I mean, are there going to be any books about your adventures as an adult? These are all my questions, thank heavens. I wish you good luck.

Magically,
Sincerely,
Christian

Dear Harry Potter,

I hope the Dursleys send you something decent for Christmas. I would be fed up if I were you, but there isn't much you can do about it, huh? I at least hope they treat you better at Hogwarts. I wish there was some way you could go and live with Sirius, but he could be sent back to Azkaban, or worse. I hope Crookshanks doesn't ever try to eat Pigwidgeon (Ron's owl). Well, I hope life will change next summer at the Dursleys.

Sincerely yours,
Katie
Brunswick, Georgia

P.S. Could you put a spell on my teacher so she wouldn't give us so much homework?

Harry Potter
Hogwarts School
England

Dear Harry,

What is Snape like? Why doesn't Snape like you? I know he's not all bad.

I know you got a letter from Hogwarts about not using your magic, but the letter said you only can use your magic if you are in big trouble. It's like let's say you were going to die with a Muggle pointing a gun right at your head and if you have a wand you can use your magic on him.

What does your scar feel like when it hurts you? Does your scar change colors when it hurts? What is the color of your scar anyway? Have you ever had a food fight at Hogwarts?

I feel sad that you don't have any parents and that the Dursleys have been so mean to you. I hope someday you can live with Sirius Black. I know you would live with anybody other than the Dursleys. The Weasleys are a nice bunch. Maybe after Lord Voldemort kicks the bucket you can live where you want.

Best regards,
Jason
Age 9
Holland, Michigan

P.S. Harry, I really love your adventures. I hope we can meet someday. I really like you! Bye!

Hi, Harry!

How are things at the moment? Hope all things are well and if not, better luck next time.

How is Potions going? Is Snape treating you more horribly than usual? He is so unfair to you, and (very obviously) favouring Malfoy.

Has Quidditch season started yet? I have never in my whole entire life heard of a more exciting sport! Flying up to fifty to 120 feet up in the air on broomsticks, bludgers rushing around, while beaters frantically shoot through everyone beating those black rockets away, chasers, scoring points, keepers, trying to keep the other team's points down, and all the while, you are sailing in and out, through the mayhem trying to catch the Snitch!

It must be such an amazing feeling to be involved in something like that. I really wish I could play Quidditch.

How is Hogwarts? Hogwarts sounds like a fabulous place to live, with all its secrets and surprises. I can't even begin to tell you what I would give to spend a day there discovering some of its mystical appearances. And what I would give to be able to sit in on one of the feasts! The food must be delicious! The house elves must be very hardworking, talented beings. (Don't tell Hermione that, though!) The meals sound so much better than what I have at home. Hogwarts is such a magical place. Well, duh! It's a school for wizards!

I have to finish now, but please say hello to Ron and Hermione for me, and I hope you get this letter. Muggle post isn't all that reliable, and I doubt they have the faintest idea where Hogwarts is!

Keep safe and don't let the Dursleys get you down!

Your friend,
Tamara
Rangiora, Canterbury
New Zealand

Interview with Tamara

I have read all of the Harry Potter books. I really like the first book compared to the others, because that's where the story begins. You are meeting the characters for the first time and discovering new places, and for me that is always exciting.

Out of all the people, I would have to say I identify the most with Ron. I don't come from an especially poor family, but sometimes we usually have to wait for things that we want, or not always have the most expensive clothes, shoes, stuff like that. I just understand where he is coming from. I have a friend who reminds me of Hermione. She is always the top in the class, and usually manages to get on the teacher's good side. But if you really need help, she is always willing, even if it involves breaking a few rules.

Reading is strongly encouraged in my family, and there is always a pile of books on our table in our hallway, from the

SYRENA
DONÉ

library. Since I first read *Harry Potter* though, I am finding it hard to find other books that can measure up. Every day I wish I could go to a place like a Hogwarts. I wish I could perform summoning charms and fly around on broomsticks. I would dearly love to go to a place like Hogwarts. Even just for a day!

I have a few things in common with Harry: We both wear glasses and have black hair that never goes or does what we want. But we both have a passion for a sport. In Harry's case, Quidditch. In my case it is cricket. Every time cricket season finishes for the year, I have an emptiness inside me until it starts again. Also Harry's age is the same as mine. I can understand and relate to what he is going through. Harry is different from me because he is a guy, and I am a girl. I know that is rather obvious, but I really can't come up with anything. Harry is just so cool! In a way I suppose, who Harry is, is the person I would like to be. Brave, kind, funny. Harry is a very, very cool guy.

I would like to see Harry finally have a loving home and family that he can go home to every holiday. Although what happens at the Dursleys' is mostly funny, I feel Harry deserves a better family and better treatment than what he gets from the Dursleys.

Dear Harry,

Hope you're doing okay. How are Ron and Hermione? Why don't you use the Body-Bind Spell (Petrificus Totalus) on your aunt and uncle and use the Tickling Charm (Rictusempra) on Dudley? How is Malfoy? (Bad I hope!) Is Snape going any easier on you? How is your Firebolt doing? Has your scar been hurting lately?

Maybe when I'm 11 I'll get to go to Hogwarts. Well, have fun. Bye!

Love,
Brian (past Headmaster at Hogwarts)
Age 9
Fremont, California

Interview with Brian

Harry Potter has made me like reading more because the books were so good, I thought maybe other books might be good, too. What I like most about Harry is what he is—magic. All my life I've loved magic, so I needed a book that was interesting and about magic.

There was this book I read called *Which Witch?* that I thought was really good, and one of my favorite characters from that book is named Arriman.

The one magic thing I'd want to use if I could is the Invisibility Cloak because I always wanted to know what it would be like to be invisible.

[As to what makes the Harry Potter books so good] I don't really know. I've read all four but I still don't know.

Dear Harry,

How is life at Hogwarts?

I wish I were a wizard or witch like you. It must be fun to be able to do magic and fly on your new Firebolt. Wow, that Firebolt really sounds like something! So how are Hermione and Ron doing? Still getting into trouble, are you? Has Sirius been sending any exciting letters lately? Well, just wanted to know how you have been lately.

Your Biggest Fan,
Tara

Hey, Harry!

How's your summer going? We hope the Dursleys aren't giving you too much trouble.

If they are, just call us, and we'll take care of them. So how are Hermione and Ron?

Hey...we were just wondering if those Bertie Bott's Every Flavor Beans are good. We almost got some but we bought a different Harry Potter item instead. Well, how's Hedwig? What about Sirius...have you heard from him lately? Very sorry about what happened to Cedric. Lord Voldemort give you any more trouble?

Man, we really wish we had powers like you. It must be really cool. Well, we think we've said enough. Tell Dumbledore we said hey.

Alwayz,
Caryn Puetz & Heather Durant
Raceland, Louisiana

P.S. Good luck w/everything!!

Dear Harry,

I love the idea of A HARRY POTTER T.V. SHOW! My Grandma is going to visit J.K. Rowling! For the book how about if Harry gets carried away and turns Dudley into a wizard?

Sincerely,
William
Tulsa, Oklahoma

Dear Harry,

I wanted to say thank you! I am profoundly amazed by your strength and bravery. You endure so much and give a voice that empowers children to handle whatever the world throws at them. Things get hard but you always seem to roll with the punches.

Tell Ron and Hermione I say "Hello." You are very lucky to have found such examples of true friendship. Reading about your life has brought magic to mine, and I am very grateful for the time I spend at Hogwarts with you. Please stay strong. It looks like things are going to get worse before they get better as your fifth year approaches, but I know you can do it, we all do.

Thanks,
Kristo
Palmdale, California

Interview with Kristo

I have read all of the Harry Potter books, and I enjoyed them very much. My favorite is *The Goblet of Fire* because Harry is really tested. He *had* to do the three tasks even though he wasn't ready in any way. Plus they were really difficult. Also, for the first time there was major friction with his friends—mainly Ron, but they worked it out. There were just so many sides to Harry that we got to see. He had to make some really tough choices like when he took Cedric back. He was faced with lots of adversity and always rose to the challenge.

I see myself as a lot like Hermione—she tries so hard to prove herself with her intelligence. I am Croatian-American and can totally identify with not fitting in fully, being different, not like everyone else. Being between two worlds. She gets flack for that, not being a pure wizard, not being like everyone else. Having this side that no one gets to ever see, it is something I identify with.

Ron and Hermione are so much like my friends. We are always together, and they are always there for me. We try to have a good time even when times are tough. There is so much trust, they're just like the characters in the book.

My friends and I bicker like the three of them. We challenge one another like the three of them.

I would love to be magical like Harry. If I was I would probably teach at Hogwarts—that would be so rad. I would like to be a Defense Against the Dark Arts professor, because they have problems keeping that position filled, and it is really important for everyone to know about. I would love to go to Hogwarts!!! In the future, I really hope that Harry becomes a Prefect.

I think Harry and I are similar when it comes to being true to ourselves. I don't think that I am the best thing since sliced bread, but when I need to do something, I do it no matter how hard it is. Challenge and conflict are just a part of life, and I think Harry and I see that as a necessary thing in order to grow. I think the main difference is that Harry is braver than I am. He is always doing something noble and brave without even trying.

I love Harry because Harry has to make decisions that are difficult and sometimes the right thing to do is not easy. I have always loved to read but the Harry Potter series has brought my love for books to a higher level.

Harry,

Waz up n.m.h? So how is Professor Lupin? Fine, I hope. So how are you? Is Mad Eye Moody still going to be the Defense

Against the Dark Arts teacher next year? Tell him I am sorry to hear what that bad guy did to him.

Are you going to stay with Ron this summer? I hope so. The Dursleys are really mean to ya. But as long as they know Sirius Black is your godfather, you shouldn't have that much trouble with them. Just remember, don't do magic out of school. 'K-well so bye.

Love always,
Your friend,
Wendie
Chowchilla, California

Dear Harry,

I'm a big fan of yours. I have read every one of your books twice, except the third and fourth books. I thought that you might like this spell, Vumerous Cracus. It sends a purple light out of the end of your wand, and your opponent's legs and arms are wrapped together. (Only in dueling!)

Why don't you want to become a Prefect like Percy when you grow up? Keep looking out for the Golden Snitch.

Your biggest fan,
Nathan
Age 10

Dear Harry,

Hogwarts. Is it like a big castle? When I read the books, I read them over and over. Every time I get a different picture of it in my head. So I was wondering what it really looked like.

Sincerely,
Grace

Dear Harry,

How's your summer been going? Did Ron really invite you stay with him sooner than usual? How was it? I suppose he didn't use Floo Powder because the Dursleys would have had him for dinner (if you know what I mean). I hope you can visit my Web site sometime. Please click on the "Harry Page" if you ever get there because that is a small blurb from your point of view. It is what I think you would say on a Web site, and you can write back telling me if it is right or how I can correct it. How was it for you and Ron and Hermione to all of a sudden find out that you were all famous in the Muggle world, too? You should've spent more time at the bookstore, huh? As you've probably guessed, I am deeply fond of your adventures at Hogwarts and really, really wish I could attend there myself. I hope you have as much fun in your fifth year as you did in your others (though due to sudden change of circumstances there is a possibility you might not).

Write back soon,
Love,
Alice

Dear Harry Potter,
How are things going at Hogwarts? Sorry that Snape is giving you such a hard time. Congratulations on almost defeating Voldemort. Are you planning on joining a big Quidditch team when you're older, and if so, what team? That's cool. How's Ron doing? How about Hermione? Well, I better not make this letter too long so I'll cut off now.

Your fan,
Steve

Dear Harry,
Hi! What's up! How's your summer? Too bad you can't play Quidditch because of the Triwizard Tournament. But it's okay since you were able to enjoy the tournament. Congratulations on your Quidditch cup and the Triwizard Tournament cup. You were really great giving the 1,000 galleons to the Weasleys. But you really deserve the money. Anyway, can I ask you a

question? Who's your favorite teacher in Hogwarts? Professor Lupin, right? Me, too. I like Professor Lupin a lot! Too bad he only lasted for one year. I really hope he'll get cured so that he can continue teaching in Hogwarts.

How does it feel studying in Hogwarts? I really think it's cool. I really want to study there with you. You should teach that Malfoy a lesson. He should not mess with you. You should cast a spell on him to make him shut up!

Well, better go. Hope to hear about your next adventure! Hope the ministry will prove that your godfather, Black, is innocent so that you can live with him and not with the Dursleys. My best regards to Ron, Hermione, and Black. Bye!

Jose
Philippines

Interview with Jose

I already read all the Harry Potter books, and I'm hoping for the fifth book.

My favorite is Book One because it introduced me to the world of Harry Potter and built a hobby. Since then I love to read all the Harry Potter books. His friends, Ron and Hermione, really remind me of my friends because they helped Harry in his problems. Ron is a Wizard by blood, while Hermione and Harry are Mudbloods. He helped them cope with the Wizarding world, which reminds me of my friends. But I can't relate to the Dursleys because I never was treated the way Harry was treated by them. My parents love me very much.

Actually I wasn't a book reader until my friend told me about Harry Potter—so, very curious about the book, I read it and liked it. So I read all four books since then. I would like to have magic because it can make my work easier. My favorite spell is the Apparate and Disapparate spell since we don't need trains and buses in transporting.

Of course I would love to study in a school like Hogwarts and make friends with people like Ron and Hermione. Maybe in some ways, Harry and I are similar. Harry is very curious in many ways, like when he wears his Invisibility Cloak to discover new things and places. I also like to explore. But maybe in a way we are quite different, because I wouldn't face a very powerful wizard if it would risk my life. I don't know, I haven't seen a wizard before. I would like to see Harry work in the Ministry of Magic because of what I've heard, that the author will stop after the seventh year when Harry will graduate. I hope she will continue writing about Harry after studying. I love Harry because, first of all, I love the genre of the story. RPG and Adventure. And secondly, I already know what his childhood and boyhood are like, so why not continue reading?

Dear Harry Potter,

How's your summer going? I bet you have a ton of homework. I was wondering what you hope your future is going to be like. I think you'd make a great Quidditch player, or even be headmaster at Hogwarts. I bet whatever you choose you'll be great at.

I also wanted to know how your friends are doing and if

you're still staying in close touch with them. Well, write me back soon.

From,
Jesse
Age 10
Dickerson, Maryland

P.S. Tell Hedwig I asked how she's doing.

Dear Harry,

I just love your books!

I started reading your books and my mom wanted to read your books to make sure they were appropriate. Of course they were! Anyway, it turned out that me and my mom were fighting over who got to read the fourth book first. Look at the time, I got to go, BYE!

Sincerely yours,
Jessica
Age 10
Colony, Texas

Interview with Jessica

Jessica is a 10-year-old from Texas who likes and admires Harry because of his bravery—but she also likes Draco Malfoy. Yes, he's bad, but as she points out, “No book is good without an enemy and a problem.” It seems having a minor, nasty character around all the time (as opposed to say, a monstrous evil like Lord “You-Know-Who” whose appearances lead to cataclysmic events) gives the book some ongoing tension, which Jessica finds intriguing.

Of course, she also likes the fun parts, like reading about Harry's flights on a broomstick—something she wishes she could try herself. (Well, don't we all!)

Despite Harry's magical gifts, what she thinks makes the character so appealing is that, in other respects, Harry is “a regular kid, and that makes him easy to relate to.”

Jessica definitely intends to keep up with the series because, in her words, “J. K. Rowling is a GREAT writer, and I can't wait to see what she comes up with.” But she's not crazy about the possibility that Harry might develop some romantic interests. “NO ROMANCE, please!” is her one suggestion to the series' author.

Dear Harry,

How's that uptight Malfoy doing! Hope he turns into a rat someday! Anyway, I made up this poem for Malfoy to tell him what I think of him. I would pay a million bucks to see the look on his face when he hears it!

Malfoy, Malfoy look at that nose!
God, don't you wash those stinky toes!
Every time I think of you,
I really feel that I will spew!

So leave Harry alone or beware,
I'll come at night and give you a scare!
We all know you're scared,
So scream for help,
'Cause when I get to you, you will go "Yelp!"

See ya later, Harry.
From Kathryn
Australia

Dear Harry,

I hope that you feel okay. I heard that your scar hurt (Hermione sent me a letter). The Dementors almost got me two days ago. I also saw Wormtail but he was with a lot of Death Eaters, and they were looking for me, so I had to hide. If you need anything just send me Hedwig.

Sincerely,
Sirius (real name: Alex)

Interview with Alex

I have read all of the books. My favorite book is Number Three, *The Prisoner of Azkaban*. I just love this book! I think it is the best one. I identify with Harry Potter because I have two close friends, a guy and a girl, and I really think that I am different than other people. Harry and I have a little bit in common, but not too much. I would love to be able to do magic. If I could do any magic I would like to Disapparate and Apparate anywhere I want. I really would like to go to a place like Hogwarts. I hope Harry falls in love with Hermione.

I love to read. I used to only read comic books but when I started to read *Harry Potter,* I started to like chapter books. I will continue to read all of the Harry Potter books.

Dear Harry,

How are you? Is school going well? I hope Snape isn't giving you too hard a time. What kind of creatures does Hagrid have in store for you this year? I hope he got rid of all the Screwts. I don't know why you put up with that Divination class. I'd quit.

I found the perfect potion to use on Malfoy! It is called Bottled Servant. First, add the skin of a boomslang, the hair of a unicorn, and bubotuber puss. Mix together well. Then add in Sleek Easy's Hair Potion and five dead spiders. Boil this with the other ingredients. This should do the trick!

Good Luck,
Laura (order of Merlin
First Class)
Moore, South Carolina

Interview with Laura

Laura gets right to the point when it comes to expressing her feelings about Harry Potter. "He's a wizard," she says.

Her second favorite character is Voldemort because "Without him there wouldn't be a story!" Next for Laura come Fred and George!

Without question, Laura would like to own a broomstick. No doubt about it—she'd like to fly.

Despite all the wizardry, Laura feels "the characters are really realistic, and you feel like you are really there!"

As for the future, Laura's views are quite adamant: "Harry and Hermione . . . yuk! . . . maybe Ron and Hermione though! [Making him an] exchange student sounds neat." But what she'd particularly like to see is more about Harry's parents: "I hope J. K. Rowling does a book about Lily and James and the other marauders." (I've heard a rumor that she'll get her wish!)

Dear Harry,

I've been meaning to write for ages, I've just been kinda busy, sorry.

HAPPY (belated) BIRTHDAY!!! Did your aunt and uncle remember? I enclose my present (I wish that I could give you something wizarding. Oh, annoying holidays), I got you a book (don't groan, you might enjoy it) for the holidays, so that you won't be so bored.

I think that Ron's going to invite us all over again, so

don't worry about how much more time you have to stay with the Dursleys.

If not, I'll see you back at Hogwarts next month.

Write back soon (PLEASE. I'm just as bored as you),

Maria
Ireland

P.S. Have you heard from Sirius and Professor Lupin yet?

Dear Harry,

I hope you know that your adventures are the best there is! I've joined HogwartsRpg's all over the Internet to feel like I go to Hogwarts, too. I like Gryffindor and Ravenclaw the best. Here's a poem about you....

Harry Potter helps you

Adventures never end

Running through the sky on broomsticks

Ravenclaw's a friend

Young but brave hearted

Putting speed on Firebolts

Opening the Chamber of Secrets

Telling others about his knowledge

Talking to Hermione and Ron

Everlasting Quidditch Seeker

Riding on a Firebolt

Phillips
Age 9
Alexandra, Virginia

Interview with Phillips

I already was an avid reader and loved to read, I couldn't put a book down! I like Harry Potter's adventures the most. He's just so interesting and cool. He always does something exciting and suspenseful in each book that won't let you put it down.

He's just like a regular kid (except he's a wizard!). He has a regular life as a Muggle but in a different school and a different world. Their day is scheduled mostly like ours: breakfast, go to school, lunch, study, snack, study, dinner, more study, sleep. He's such a neat kid though, even though some people are jealous like Draco Malfoy and his gang. (He's also an excellent Quidditch player!)

My favorite character isn't Harry Potter, however. Hermione is. Hermione is smart just like me. She's a good student, funny, and sassy sometimes. My second favorite character is Harry though.

If I could use one spell or magic item from *Harry Potter* it would be either a Firebolt or a Learn How to Do Spells Kit that comes with a special wand made just for you!

I think children like *Harry Potter* so much because it's just so different from the stuff Muggle kids do. WE can't fly on broomsticks play Quidditch, go to magic classes, or learn how to do magic! It's every kid's fantasy world. Harry is such a wonderful character because he is a hero, an imaginative kid, and he gets picked on, like many other Muggles do.

My advice for J. K. Rowling is that she shouldn't make Hermione have a romance with Harry Potter. I think Dudley should find out that Harry is a famous wizard and look up stuff on him and find out who his blood brother really is (maybe that will make him appreciate Harry much more). I also think that there should be a new broom, a competitor of the Firebolt, that has the same speed and tricks, except it comes with more free stuff with it, and costs much less than a Firebolt, but it has a minor glitch: It stops working in its first month of use. This broom should be called the Lightning Bolt! When you peel off the sticker that has the Lightning Bolt seal on it, it says underneath Cheap-O Nimbus 1000. Then this broom scam is posted on the front cover of the *Daily Prophet.* All of the Hogwarts students who bought the broom, and their parents are trying to sue the Cheap-O joke company, and it causes a riot with the Ministry of Magic. I think that Draco Malfoy will buy the broom first and brag about how much better it is compared to the Firebolt, then two weeks later his broom doesn't work anymore!

If there is a soundtrack for the movie *Harry Potter and the Sorcerer's Stone,* one of the songs should be:

Artist: M2M
Album:Shades of Purple
Song: Pretty Boy

I think the song "Pretty Boy" should be put in the soundtrack for Cedric Diggory. It sounds magical, and it sounds like Cedric Diggory and a Chang Cho romance.

Dear Harry,

How's everything at Hogwarts? I hope you, Ron, Hermione, and the rest of your friends are well. (That includes Sirius and Hedwig.) You were really good at the Triwizard Tournament. Congratulations!

It must be really fun to play Quidditch. I wish I could play, but mind you, I'd probably get sick. Have any new broom-sticks come out yet that are better than the Firebolt? Is Snape any easier on you? And is Malfoy still very mean? (He probably is.) Has Dudley lost any weight yet? (He probably hasn't.) He'll make himself really sick if he doesn't lose any weight (serves him right, he's such a spoiled brat. He must have inherited his meanness from Uncle Vernon and Aunt Petunia.).

Harry, here is a Sleep Potion you might find useful:

Ingredients

A quarter of a cup of dragon's blood

1 unicorn hair

3 crocodile fangs

1 cup of apple juice

the snore of a gnome

a flame from a dragon
the roar of a lioness

Method

1. Combine dragon's blood, crocodile fangs, and apple juice into a cauldron and stir.
2. Add the snore of a gnome.
3. Now add the rest of the ingredients but leave the unicorn hair till last.
4. After the unicorn hair is put in, do not stir.

The Sleep Potion is now complete, perhaps you can force-feed it to Percy when he starts yakking about stuff. I'm afraid I can't send this by owl but I hope you don't mind me sending it to you by Muggle post. (It might be a bit slower than owl post.) Good luck to you in the future!

Sincerely,
Breeann
Age 11
Lismore, NSW
Australia

Dear Harry Potter,

How are you getting along with your two best friends, Ron Weasley and Hermione Granger? Are you trying to teach

Neville Longbottom to try and remember the passwords to the common room? Hope you're keeping Malfoy under control and showing off your new Firebolt. You are so lucky that you get to fly on a broomstick and use a wand to do magic.

Are you glad Hagrid came and picked you up from your aunt and uncle's house? You were probably really excited when you heard you were a wizard and you could go to Hogwarts and do magic.

What is your favourite class at Hogwarts? I bet it isn't Potions with Snape. Albus Dumbledore is probably going nuts over trying to find replacement teachers for the Defence Against the Dark Arts class. I think that class is jinxed!

Well, hope you have fun playing the best sport in the wizarding world... Quidditch!

I also hope you win the Quidditch cup and the House cup again!

Sincerely,
Tawnya
Canada, BC

Dear Harry,

How did you first feel when you became a wizard? Were you a little scared about going to Hogwarts? I know you were afraid you wouldn't fit in at Hogwarts and that you weren't even sure you could be a wizard, although Hagrid had convinced you. How did you feel when you first met Ron, and why didn't you want anybody to know who you were? And at Christmas in your first year, why didn't you want Fred and George to know about the Invisibility Cloak?

Also, I wanted to tell you that you are my favorite person in the whole world. I may be a Muggle, but I still know about you. Your parents would be proud about the wizard you've become. I can't wait to see what happens next. I'm watching you.

Your Unknown Friend,
Lindsay
Age 12

Dear Harry Potter,

What's it like to be a famous wizard? Well, it must be stupendously awesome!

Anyway, I'm 10. I have three dogs. My favorite animals are wolves, horses, and dragons.

I admire your books. I dressed up as Hermione for Halloween. I know about a new spell called Leave Me Be, and all you have to say is "Leave me be." Then an extremely large lightning bolt comes down on whomever you want!

You are sooooo lucky! I like to pretend that I live in a

SYRENA
DONÉ

place where mystical animals like dragons, unicorns, and phoenixes live.

Sincerely,
Acacia
Arkansas

P.S. Can you give me some tips on Quidditch and wizardry?

Interview with Acacia

Has reading Harry Potter *made you enjoy reading even more? Why?*
Reading *Harry Potter* has encouraged me to read more because it's just such an excellent book that it makes you think there may be other great books out there.

What do you like most about Harry Potter?
What I enjoy most about *Harry Potter* is how Harry just can't keep out of trouble and is so adventuresome.

After Harry, who is your second (or third) favorite character? Why?
Hedwig is my second favorite character because she is always so proud, noble, and loyal. Whenever Pigwiggin or another owl takes his place she always has to ignore him for a few days.

If you could use just one spell or magical item from Harry Potter, *what would it be?*
I'd say Harry's map of Hogwarts, because then I could see when Elias (my twin brother) steals cookies.

Why do you think children love reading about Harry Potter so much? What makes Harry Potter *such a wonderful book and character?*
Kids like me love reading Harry Potter books because the entire book is an adventure. The way J. K. Rowling wrote it draws us into the book and makes us feel like we're there. *Harry Potter* is full of adventure. When you think your parents are mean and then you read *Harry Potter,* you see how good you have it.

Do you have any advice for J. K. Rowling about future books? Should Harry Potter's friendship with Hermione turn romantic? Or should he try a year as an exchange student in an American school of witchcraft and wizardry? Any ideas?
Here's my advice for J. K. Rowling: Keep up the fantastic work! About Harry and Hermione, well, maybe, but it's up to J. K. Rowling. I'll read whatever she writes. Harry could try to be an exchange student in America or someone in America could be an exchange student to Hogwarts.

Dear Harry,

Meet me at 3:00 P.M. at the edge of the forbidden forest close to the Quidditch field.

From,
Samantha

Dear Harry Potter,

My name is Nicholas. I'm in fourth grade, and I have red hair and freckles. How did you feel about going to Hogwarts? I have read the first and second books. They were great. I think you are good at being a seeker in Quidditch. What teacher at Hogwarts do you like best? Do you miss your parents? I'm sorry for what happened to your parents. What other sport do you like?

Sincerely,
Nick

Dear Harry,

I thought it was funny when you, Ron, and Hermione blasted Snape into the wall. I hope your Firebolt is in shape. Who is going to be the new Defense Against the Dark Arts teacher this year? I wonder when the next book is going to come out.

One of your biggest
fans around,
Logan

Dear Harry,

How's Quidditch? I hope it's going good. How's Sirius Black, and have you been seeing him?

From,
Sean

P.S. Please send back the answers for these questions.

Dear Harry Potter,

How are you doing? Harry, please tell me what you remember from Voldemort killing your parents. Why don't you ask Snape? Why doesn't he like you? I mean it's only a question. Are the Dursleys still being mean to you? I hope not. I have your first and second book. I can't wait to find out who is turning the students to stone! I think all of your books are great! Bye, maybe I'll see you at Hogwarts!

From,
Heather

Dear Harry Potter,

I am one of your biggest fans, but I am not big like Dudley. I have two, no, wait, three questions about Hogwarts' teachers: Is Minerva McGonagall married? Is Albus Dumbledore in love with Minerva? And why is Snape so mean to you and all the Gryffindors instead of all the Slytherins? I also think you should marry Ginny, and then you and Ron can be brothers, and then Ron can marry Hermione, then all you guys can be family. But for now just be yourself and have fun being friends. Got to go!

In friendship,
Miranda

Dear Harry,

How is Hogwarts? I think it's really cool that you can be a wizard! Did you suspect [name deleted] before he revealed himself [at the end of the first book]? Is Malfoy driving you crazy? If so, use this spell to make him send love letters to Pansy Parkinson:

Idiotic, stupid Malfoy
Send some letters to your lover boy
Parkinson won't like that
You're dirtier than the Sorting Hat!
(But definitely not as smart!)

Has Neville lost Trevor recently? When Fred and George set up their joke shop, use some of their trick wands on the

Slytherins. Won any Quidditch matches lately? Have a great year!

Sincerely,
Alex (wizard-to-be)
Age 10
Potomac, Maryland

Dear Harry Potter,

You are so lucky that you can fly. How does it feel when you are flying? You are also lucky that you know magic. One day I hope that I can do magic, too!

Maybe one day we can have a duel.

Your Admirer,
Julian (Expert Wizard)
Potomac, Maryland

Dear Harry,

You are the greatest wizard I have ever heard of. I admire you very much, and I wish I could go to the Hogwarts School of Wizardry because I would so much like to meet you and get to know you. My name is Lily, and I am a beautiful 16-year-old enchantress with long silver hair and piercing gray eyes. My favourite color is blue, so I usually wear lovely bright blue silk robes and a pair of silver shoes to match my hair. From time to time, when I go to a party, I create a magic sparkle around myself to make me look even more beautiful. I would send you my photo but I am afraid that I would walk off the frame too often, as I am very lively. I like music and poetry (actually, I learn them in my school besides the magic classes).

I go to the QueLynn School of Magic Arts, which is very far in the North. It is actually a beautiful ice castle on the endless snowy fields, and our headmistress Lyana Van Heeusen is a true snow queen.

I go to the sixth class, and I am a bright student (like Hermione, I guess), because I love magic very much. Like Hogwarts we also have different houses, though in our school, there are three houses. I have been sorted to the house of Heeliya, which unites the enchanters and enchantresses who are bright-witted. There is also the house of Zoefinn for the brave and adventurous students, and the house of Candeon, which is like the house of Slytherin in your school. The students in Candeon are usually malignant, and I don't like them very much, but I have many friends in the other two houses. I like to learn, and the class of spells is without doubt my favourite. I already know so many cool spells. I can even teach you one of my favourites. Here it is:

Out of the hazy blue sky
And the endless mind

Make a poem appear
In the sweet-scented air.

This spell creates a poem in the air. Just wave with your magic wand and say the spell, and the poem should appear just in front of you in the silver and blue sparkle. And the best thing about this spell is that it always creates a different poem that matches your mood perfectly and makes you feel better when you are sad or tired, or it expresses your joy. Sometimes the spell even creates special effects, like fireworks or music, but only when your feelings are strong enough.

I invented this spell, and I have used it many times. I hope that you like it.

Do you like magical creatures? I love them, and especially the unicorn. My dream is to own one of those charming creatures, but there are so few of them in the far North. I have read that our climate is too harsh for them. But I still have some pets. First of all I own two most beautiful northern butterflies. They are very fragile, soft, and shiny creatures. I keep them in a little silver cage in my room. Sometimes I wear them in my hair where they change colour and wave their wings beautifully all the time. They are called Shyn and Shain, and I have had them for eleven years already. I also have a snow-white owl just like yours, only mine has a little bright blue ribbon around its left leg. I call my owl Iris, and I love her very much. I would send my letter to you with her, only she is on her way to Norway right now. She is taking a letter to my best friend who is called Laurel Fayhill. Laurel is an enchantress, too, and she is very clever and kindhearted. She goes to the Blue Fjords School of Magic.

I am so worried about you, Harry!!! You are in a great danger now that Lord Voldemort is back. He certainly wants to destroy you. I think you are so brave, and I wish you all the luck for your next school year!!! Have fun!!!

Love,
Sigrid (this is the name that I use in the world of Muggles, but my real name is Lilly)
Viljandi, Estonia

P.S. Give my greetings to Ron and Hermione. They are very good friends, and you are so lucky to know them! I hope that you will all be alright.

P.P.S. You know, I play Quidditch, too, and I am also a seeker. I think it is such a cool game, don't you? I love to ride a broom, and I always enjoy the excitement of competing.

Dear Harry,

How did you first feel when you became a wizard? Were you a little scared about going to Hogwarts? I know you were afraid you wouldn't fit in at Hogwarts and that you weren't even sure you could be a wizard, although Hagrid had convinced you. How did you feel when you first met Ron, and why didn't you want anybody to know who you were?

And at Christmas in your first year, why didn't you want Fred and George to know about the Invisibility Cloak?

Also, I wanted to tell you that you are my favorite person in the whole world. I may be a Muggle, but I still know about you. Your parents would be proud about the wizard you've become. I can't wait to see what happens next. I'm watching you.

Your Unknown Friend,
Jasmel (Jason and Melissa)

Dear Harry,

I absolutely love your adventures. They are so cool. I wish I were you but I'm just a 12-year-old girl who is a dreamer. I dream about being a witch so I could get revenge on a few people very similar to Draco Malfoy and his cronies. I really like how you disarmed Professor Snape in your third year-it was so good.

Say hello to Ron and Hermione for me, as they are also as important as you. I hope Sirius and Buckbeak are okay and Professor Dumbledore, too.

Do you need more spells, as I am more than willing to help? Maybe this spell will help you to defeat the ever-powerful

Voldemort. My friends told me it. It's El Kasa Di Mi for Ka. It's supposed to weaken your opponents before they weaken you, then you can kill them—that's if you want to. It might even be useful against Malfoy.

Hope everyone is well. Is Percy Weasley still so bigheaded about his job as a P.A. at the Ministry? Have you suggested a Peggaguas to Hagrid yet, as they make good pets? I hope he is well. Oh, well, I gotta go. Please write back soon.

Love,
Rebecca
Age 12
Sydney, Australia

Dear Harry Potter,

How are you doing?

I'm doing just fine, only I'm going mad waiting for the fifth book about you to come out.... It's driving me insane!!!

I hope you find [name deleted] soon so then you can go and live with Sirius Black. How great would that be... leaving the Dursleys forever.

I'd send you a butterbeer, only it'd go everywhere while in the post, but the next time you have a Butterbeer... think of me.

I hope you are finding things to keep you busy. How's Hedwig? Well, I really should go now because I want to re-read *The Goblet of Fire*!!!

Love,
Jacqui
Age 12
Victoria, Australia

P.S. Say "Hi!" to Ron and Hermione for me. Oh, and good luck to all of you!!!

Interview with Jacqui

Jacqui's always been an enthusiastic reader, but she adds that the Harry Potter books "have made me enjoy my reading even more."

She loves all the magical elements in the books equally, or at least so well that when asked which one she would most like to have, answered, "EVERYTHING!!!"

She loves Harry, of course, but her second favorite character is not the most popular answer (Hermione, according to my informal survey) but the more offbeat choice of Hagrid. Why, I asked, and she told me, "because he is so funny—not to mention tall. I also think it's funny that he loves dangerous animals." I can tell she sympathizes with him, because she goes on to add, "Poor Hagrid. He hasn't had much luck with keeping all of them though, has he?"

Her third favorite characters are Fred and George. Again I ask why, and again she says, "They're funny!"

Jacqui clearly is a girl who appreciates the humor in the series. But she likes the adventure, too—especially the flying broomsticks. If she could have any of Harry Potter's magical possessions, that's the one she'd go for. What she'd do first is "soar through the air, with the wind in my hair. The views would be fantastic, and I could go anywhere I wanted to."

That's also a large part of why she thinks *Harry Potter* has been such a success. "I think other children love reading *Harry Potter* because they love dreaming about those sorts of things, and they know that maybe, just maybe, one day they might really happen. We may have flying broomsticks, Butterbeers, and The Hogwarts School of Witchcraft and Wizardry. Hey, anything can happen!"

Well, of course, in your imagination, that's true right now!

Dear Harry,

I am really proud of you! Especially when there is a movie- all about you! Wow! Anyway, I think your aunt and uncle will respect you more if you help Dudley with his weight lifting! I hope Sirius Black has cleared his name. That way, you don't have to stay with your aunt and uncle, and you will enjoy your holidays!

Love,
Regina
Age 11
Singapore

Interview with Regina

Regina is an 11-year-old girl who lives in Singapore. She says that the Harry Potter books have definitely helped her to improve her reading. I asked in what way, and she explained: "*Harry Potter* is so interesting, that after reading it I continued to look out for interesting books like *Harry Potter!* Now reading is definitely my hobby! Especially reading *Harry Potter!*"

Here's what she likes most about the schoolboy wizard: "Other than his scar, it's that he really has sportsmanship!"

But after Harry, it's tough for Regina to decide who's her favorite character. "I can't decide!" she moans. "Fred? George? Ron? Hermione . . . I love them all! But I think I'll pick Professor Dumbledore, because without him, none of the books would end up with a happy ending."

As for a favorite power—one that she'd like to have herself—she was about to give me one of the more popular responses, the Invisibility Cloak, and then she remembered something no other child thought to mention: "Oh, Sleekeazy's Hair Potion. I need to smooth my bushy hair!"

But magic potions and cloaks and flying broomsticks alone can't account for the success of the series, according to Regina. She thinks it's the entire imagined world of Hogwarts that draws kids in and keeps them hooked. "It's so cool, and I guess most children like to pretend it's real."

The following letters are from the second grade in Columbia Academy in Columbia, Tennessee. Pretty good writing from a bunch of seven- and eight-year-olds! Thanks to Becky Spears for asking her class to send in these letters.

Dear Harry Potter,

I wish I had a broom so I could fly around my school. I hope Snape is not so mean next year. I hope you have a nice year with Sirius Black. I hope you kill the murderer who framed Black.

Your Friend,
Paul
Columbia, Tennessee

Dear Harry,

You are so lucky because you get to ride on a broom! I wish I could meet you. I wish you could do magic at home so you could turn Dudley into a lump of coal. Here's a potion for you to put in your book:

A drop of vinegar, one strip of cloth,
A cooked rabbit, and broken glass.

This will make Dudley turn into a pig, even though he already acts like one.

How is Hermione doing? I sure hope Malfoy isn't spoiling

your fun. My mom doesn't like your school, but she loves your books! I sure hope Snape isn't holding a grudge.

Love,
Erika
Springhill, Tennessee

Dear Harry,

I hope I can meet you someday! I love all your friends and all the people at Hogwarts. I hope you aren't too sad about your parents because I miss them, too. I hope you have a good time at Hogwarts. I am looking forward to your next book.

Your friend,
Ryan
Columbia, Tennessee

Dear Harry Potter,

I hope I get to meet you someday. I love you and your friends so much!

Your Friend,
Rebekah
Columbia, Tennessee

Dear Harry,

I love all your books! I am looking forward to your next book. I hope Sirius Black is innocent because I want you to live with him. Harry, I hope Lupin comes back.

Love,
Sam
Columbia, Tennessee

Dear Harry,

I hope the Dursleys do not drive you crazy when you are at their house. I hope you have a good time at their house. I hope you call Ron and see if he can pick you up in his flying car. I hope next year you win the World Cup, and I hope you sign up for Quidditch also.

Love,
Hunter
Culleoka, Tennessee

Dear Harry Potter,

Do you want to cast a spell on Malfoy? I bet you do! He is so mean to you!

I know you can't use magic outside of Hogwarts. Why is the scar on your head shaped like a lightning bolt? I hope you are able to kill Lord Voldemort and his servant, so he cannot give Lord Voldemort any more power!

Love,
Reybekka
Columbia, Tennessee

Dear Harry,

It must be fun to do magic! Do you like to ride a broom? I think it would be fun to ride a broom. Do you like your godfather? I hope he is nice to you. Is the Invisibility Cloak cool? I like the name of this book, *Kids' Letters to Harry Potter.* If I ever meet you, I hope you can teach me some tricks. Do you like Ginny? Is Ron your best friend?

Your friend,
Trey
Columbia, Tennessee

Dear Harry,

I hope this year is a great year for you at Hogwarts! I want to know if your Firebolt (broomstick) will try to buck you off again? When you go to live with Sirius Black, I want to know if he is nice to you! How does it feel to be famous?

Love,
Rachel
Columbia, Tennessee

Dear Harry Potter,

Has Ron broken his wand again? Has Peeves stopped being so mean to everyone?

I think you are very good at Quidditch. Do you think they will ever chop down the whomping willow?

Your Friend,
Noah
Columbia, Tennessee

Dear Harry Potter,

How do you like living with the Dursleys? Maybe you can put a spell on Dudley to make him be your servant! I think your school should have a new class, Defense Against Dangerous Creatures. How is it having a fake criminal for a godfather?

Your Friend,
Kegan
Columbia, Tennessee

Dear Harry Potter,

Have you learned where the Ravenclaws' or Hufflepuffs' common room is? Are you going to go in the Ravenclaws' common room in your fifth year at Hogwarts? The Marauders' Map might help you find the Ravenclaws' or Hufflepuffs' common room. When you do find the common rooms, you need to go in and take the Polyjuice Potion.

Your Friend,
Spencer
Columbia, Tennessee

Dear Harry Potter,

Do you ever see the head dragon? Do you ever see giant spiders? Do you ever see seven-headed dragons? Do you ever see lizards? I really love all your books!

Your Friend,
Brennan
Columbia, Tennessee

Dear Harry Potter,

Why are your aunt and uncle so mean? Why do you have a godfather? Do you like your godfather? I hope he is not mean to you.

Love,
Jessica
Springhill, Tennessee

Dear Harry,

How is Quidditch going? Have you caught the Golden Snitch lately? How is Sirius? Is Buckbeak okay? Oh yeah, how is Hagrid and the Nifflers, too? How are Ron and Hermione? Did [name deleted] get killed yet? Tell me if anything comes up about school.

Yours sincerely,
Nash
Springhill, Tennessee

To Harry Potter:

I know you despise staying at the Dursleys' during the summer holiday, but it's for your own good! (How many times has an adult witch or wizard told you that?) After all, Dumbledore used ancient magic that prevents Voldemort from harming you while at the Dursleys'! But even so, it is horrible that you have to stay at the Dursleys' house! They treat you like some animal with a disease (like Mad Cow or sometlting).

On to lighter topics. How's Hedwig? Sometimes I wonder if she's like a Minerva McGonagall in disguise! The disapproval she showed during the incident with the flying car (yes, yes! I know you don't want to hear about it again!) was so similar in attitude! Ohhh! I can't wait to see what broom comes out next! What could be better then a Firebolt? What I really want to know though, is (drumroll please!; puts on Game Show host voice) "Who Will be the next Defense Against the Dark Arts teacher? Stay Tuned!"

I really like Dumbledore. As you have said, he probably does know everything that goes around in Hogwarts! What sets him apart from the other teachers is he only tells you what to do or answers your questions when you need to know. Like for instance, we are all still pondering on why Voldermort was after your parents in the first place! One day we'll know!

I love the sound of *Every Flavour Beans* and think that while some flavours like *Ear Wax* are GROSS!!!, it would be so much fun and would be a laugh whenever someone got a disgusting flavour.

From,
Jade
Cairns, Australia

P.S. Sorry, I couldn't use Owl post as it would attract to much attention! E-owl was as close as I could get! Oh . . . and say hello to Sirius and Buckbeak for me!

Dear Harry Potter,

How are you feeling? That was a close shave with Voldemort you had this year. Don't feel guilty about your rival's death; it could happen to anyone. I hope you get to spend at least one week of summer vacation with Sirius. I wonder what mission Dumbledore sent him to do.

Have you received any owls from Ron and Hermione? I hope they are having a good summer. Harry, I wanted to tell

SYRENA DONE

you what a very generous thing it was that you gave the Weasley twins the winnings you got in the Triwizard Tournament. Sorry, but I can't send this letter by owl post because I don't have an owl.

Best wishes for your
fifth year.
Marisabel
Age 14
Los Angeles, California

Dear Harry Potter,

You are really cool! You are my hero! You kicked Voldemort's butt! You rock! Hopefully, you and Hermione finally admit you two like each other! Good luck kicking Voldemort's butt again!

Sincerely,
Nancy

Dear Harry,

You always seem to have a lot of adventures so I guess I wanted to tell you that you handle them very well!

I mean the Triwizard Tournament broke me in half! You definitely deserved to win, but in the end it was all a mean, dirty trick.

I hope things are going well for you, Ron, and Hermione. Tell Hermione if she has problems with her curly hair to get in touch with me-I have the same problem!

Love,
Polly
Seaforth Simon's Town
South Africa

P.S. I think Voldemort is pond scum!

Interview with Polly

Polly was already "a dedicated reader" when the first Harry Potter book came out. To prove it she told me she owns more than 400 books!

What set *Harry Potter* apart from other books in her mind was the "magicalness" and the mystery of the books. The series is "one of a kind." And as an author, "J. K. rocks!"

When I asked about other favorite characters, Polly was quick to tell me who she *didn't* like: Hermione (strange, because she seemed to be most girls' favorite!), but Polly was quick to point to the reason: "She's too prim!" But she does like Dumbledore and Sirius.

When it comes to magic equipment, Polly's hands-down winner was the flying broomstick. Like most kids she's imagined herself on a Firebolt, after reading about Harry's flights. "I'd love the feeling of being able to fly and look down . . . amazing!"

"Might you ever get tired of *Harry Potter*?" I asked. To which Polly promptly shot back, "I wish there was one every month. I'd spend all my pocket money! J. K. is super!"

She's got some good ideas of her own about some new adventures that Ms. Rowling could use in the next book in the series. "I think J. K. should let him fly away for a few weeks and go on safari [to South Africa, I'm assuming, which is where Polly lives]. Harry should make Voldemort grow warts on his head!"

Dear Harry,

How are you? How's Hogwarts? How are your lessons? You know you are lucky that you go to such an amazing school. Mine is so boring that if you go to sleep, you're bound to stay asleep till the end of the day.

I need advice on how to tackle people like Malfoy and Dudley. There are a couple of kids in my class who are like that. They are pains in the neck.

I love your broom, and I love Quidditch (even though I can't play it!). If I ever get to meet you, will you please allow me touch the broom, if not ride it? Or just a glimpse of it would do.

I don't have an owl, but I do have a faint idea on how to get this letter to you. Please would you accept my apologies for this?

Sincerely,
Simrat
Age 12
New Delhi, India

P.S. Could you talk to Professor Dumbledore and find out if I'm on the list for Hogwarts? I'm going to be 11 soon.

Interview with Simrat

Reading to me has always been fun, but while I read *Harry Potter* I've had a lot more fun than I used to have. In *Harry Potter* you can really imagine all the passages right down to every nook and cranny. Each page yields a thrilling adventure that makes you want to keep on reading.

I like the thrill and mystery that J. K. Rowling adds to the whole novel, leaving it incomplete so that it forms a chain with the sequels of the particular book you're reading in the Harry Potter series.

I like the portrayal of loyal friends, too. Ron and Hermione are both great characters who seem to stick up for Harry even in the worst of times.

I like the magical items, but if I could have just one, I would pick the magic wand so that I can heal the world of its bad things, and also so that I could do well in all aspects of school.

What makes Harry special, it seems to me, is that he is the boy who survived. He doesn't know at first that he's a wizard, so whatever happens in the book, he doesn't usually know much more than any other kid, because of his lack of knowledge of magic. And also, he is underage. It's easy to understand how he feels.

I think J. K. Rowling just has to keep on writing as well as she's writing right now to keep up the quality of the series. I wouldn't guess where the characters might go from here. I'd rather let the books take their own course.

Dear Harry,

How's life at Hogwarts?? Have you been able to talk to Cho lately?? Has Snape been treating you any worse?? What's your favorite class at Hogwarts? It's probably Flying class, right? Not that you NEED lessons on flying. You're a natural. My brother is EXACTLY LIKE DUDLEY. That's like the only way I can relate to you, except that you don't have a brother (wish I didn't). He annoys me, he's as fat as a pig, and he follows me everywhere. If you ever find a spell to get rid of or change Dudley in any way, can you send it to me?? Thanks. Say hi to Ron and Hermione for me. Good luck in the future, Harry!!!

Bye!!!
Shavika
Hyattsville, Maryland

Interview with Shavika

Harry Potter really did change my attitude toward reading. I didn't really like reading very much, but then my cousin told me about the Harry Potter books and convinced me to read the first one. I did, and now I have all four books so far. It also made me read some other books.

What I like most about *Harry Potter* is that the books have so many twists, and you never know what's going to happen next. J. K. Rowling really keeps you guessing!

After Harry, my favorite character is Ron, because he and Harry always get into mischief, and it's fun to know what's going to happen to them. Next, I like Hermione, because she helps Harry and Ron a lot and is a good friend.

If I could have any of the magic items from the books, I would like to use a wand, because it's what you can make magic with, and it would be fun.

I'm not sure why the books have been such a hit. . . . Lots of writers have written books about magic and things like that, but J. K. Rowling made her books the kind that you just can't put down as soon as you start reading them, and then pretty soon you've read the whole series. Harry Potter is a good character because it's fun to learn about his life and things. The reason people also like the books is that the books are in a boarding school as a setting, and that's unusual for kids these days to read about.

Dear Harry Potter,

Hello.

Can you please help me learn the Polyjuice Potion? I would really like to 'cause it looks like fun. Could you also give me any other potion recipes and spells??

Is Hedwig happy? And Ron and Pigwidgeon? And Hermione and Crookshanks? And Sirius and Buckbeak? Hope they are.

Anyway . . . Buh Bye.
M. G.

The following letters are from the Kreamer Street Primary School in Bellport, New York.

Dear Harry,

I am so excited to meet you. I read the fourth book. It was so cool. Harry, will you ever trust Professor Lupin because if he is a werewolf I would stay away from him. Hey, Harry, I liked it when you stopped the Whomping Willow. Harry, I liked it when you won the Quidditch Cup. Harry, how's Hedwig? It was a little scary when Sirius Black dragged Ron around when his leg was broken. Harry, it was so nice talking to you.

Your friend,
Jeffrey

Dear Harry,

I like all your books. You write the best books I ever read. Can you send me a picture of the owl? I like the book with the owl in the front. I might like your fifth book.

Your friend,
Joseph

Dear Harry,

Hi! How are you? I am so excited to be writing to you. How are all of your friends? I am reading Book Number Three. It is starting to get cool. How many books do you think J.K. Rowling will write? You and Hedwig are my favorite characters in all the books. I hope you are learning a lot at Hogwarts. I always wanted to be able to fly on a broomstick just like you. Is it fun? I started your first book but I never finished. Well, I wish I could talk more but I have to go.

Your friend,
Taylor

P.S. Watch out for Sirius Black.

Dear Harry,

Hi, Harry! I've read your books-they're great! I want to tell you a potion that I have thought up. It is called Disease. It will be for science. Hermione and Ron would like it. What does Sirius Black look like? Did you and Ron ever get in a big fight? I bet the next book will be great, just like all the other ones. I love in the third book where you meet Sirius Black toward the end of the book. Scabbers is on Sirius Black's chest. That was funny. Hope you like my letter.

Your friend,
Jennifer

Dear Harry,

Hi, Harry! I like your books. Do you like your Firebolt? You should try to be a licensed animagus. Here's some new spells: "Magneto"-it lets you move metal objects. "Vulcan Lance"-it melts things. "Change-o"-it changes things. "Amos Wand"-it calls your wand back.

Your friend,
Nicholas

Dear Harry,

Hello, Harry. How are you doing? I love your books. They're very interesting. Love Book Three. I'm reading it right now. In some chapters it's very scary. You're very brave. Who is your favorite friend? I like Hermione because she's smart, and I'm smart, too. I do like you, too. Do you like Hogwarts? Just wanted to tell you I'm very sad that your mom and dad died. Were you scared when Sirius Black almost got your friend? Weren't you sad? I like your first book best. I'm glad you won the Quidditch game. It was so close but that was a good idea about your plan to win Quidditch. I can't wait till your next book comes out. I bet it's going to be better than ever. I can't wait to read the rest of the book. I wonder what's going to happen to Scabbers and Sirius Black and the other people. I would like to go to Hogwarts, too, to learn to do magic. It seems very cool to learn magic. Well, it's nice talking to you. Maybe you can write back to me and answer the questions. Bye, see you later.

Your fan,
Mariah

Dear Harry,

Hello, Harry. I would love to ask you a few questions like why do you play on the Gryffindor team. Maybe you could make up your own spells, like to be able to freeze things.

I loved all of your books. How are Ron and Hermione? I hope Professor Snape is not being so mean. I hope you are enjoying your year at Hogwarts. I had a great time writing to you.

Sincerely,
Chapell

Dear Harry,

Hey, Harry. How are you doing? I am so happy to see you. I was just going to tell you a new spell that you can use when Voldemort tries to get you. To do the spell you have to say, "Evil wizard," then he'll go away and never come back. Isn't it great?

Your friend,
Nereida

Dear Harry,

How are you? I have read three of your books. I have just a few questions for you: Were you afraid Sirius Black was going to kill you? I would be very scared. I liked the third book the best. How is Hagrid? Does he know what you and Hermione did to save Buckbeak?

Snape is not that nice, is he? He does not like you. Lupin likes you except when you had the Marauders' Map. When I read the third book I found out that Lupin is a [plot detail omitted] and your father was [another plot detail omitted], too. I think you were amazed. Well, it was nice to write.

Your fan,
Brittany

Dear Harry,

I'm such a fan of your books. How about a new spell called Shield-Magno? It makes a shield around you, and it has a magnet so you can take another person's wand. Hey! How about a new book called *How to Teleport*? Cool, huh? How about an electronic owl? It delivers mail and receives at 101 mph.

Your number one fan,
Stephen

Dear Harry,

I may be able to give you a new spell! A spell that can teleport you so when Voldemort tries to kill you, you can get away. Where did you get that wand? And I got another spell for you. A spell that has an invisible bomb!!!!!

Your friend,
Esteban

Dear Harry,

How do you do your magic? I can't believe that I'm writing to you. I hope in the next book that you win the Quidditch match. What is it like in Hogwarts? Is it fun playing with your friend Ron? Watch out for Sirius Black! I hope Hedwig isn't hurt or in pain. She's a good pet to you, probably. I know you have to like sports because of your Quidditch match. I like sports, too. Do you know that Professor Lupin has turned into a [surprise deleted]? I believe Dumbledore is a nice headmaster of the school. If I ever see you in real life I want to see your magic. I just hope you don't find Voldemort, the evil wizard.

Your friend,
April

Dear Harry,

Hi! How are you and Hedwig? I like Hedwig a lot, and of course you, too. Are the Dementors scary in real life? They look pretty funny. You are so lucky to be in books. What is it like being in Hogwarts? I myself like magic. I am sure you do, too. You are so cool. What is it like being on the Quidditch team? I love sports.

Is Professor Snape really that mean to you? I wish I could meet you in person but I can't. Oh yeah, how are Hermione and Ron? What is it like having magic? Well, anyway, I just want you to know I am your biggest FAN!

Love,
Ashley

Dear Harry,

I like you because you are friendly. Why do you want to be a wizard? Can you turn back into a baby? That would be cool.

Why did your mom and dad die? I hope they went to heaven.

Why does Professor Snape have his nails painted? How many months does it take to be a wizard?

Your friend,
Kevin

Dear Harry,

Why are you so afraid of the Dementors? I'm your number one fan. Is Sirius Black going to die? How old were your parents when they died? How many spells do you know?

Your friend,
William

Dear Harry,

I think it's really cool to have an Invisibility Cloak. I would love to have one. It also must have been fun to be in the Quidditch final. I wonder if you were scared when you faced Voldemort. I would be scared. How is your Firebolt holding up?

How is your godfather doing? Is he out of Azkaban?

Your friend,
Andrew

Dear Harry,

Hi, Harry. How are you doing? Are you doing fine at Hogwarts? I hope so. Are you still 11 years old, and are you still in England? I am having fun at Kreamer Street School.

Did you learn how to do magic yet? I like that white owl. It is pretty. I wish I could learn magic. Are you learning new spells, and are you making new books? Hope you will write back.

Your friend,
Leeann

Dear Harry,

Harry, how are you? I have been reading your books, and I like them. I enjoy them very much, and I dream that I am there. I wish that you could come and play with me and be my friend.

Your friend,
Love,
Monet

Editor's warning: Don't read the next letter if you haven't already read Harry Potter and the Goblet of Fire. *The letter writer describes much of the plot, including the ending, which would spoil the fun for anyone who doesn't already know what happens!*

Dear Harry,

In your fourth year you had a lot of problems with the Triwizard Tournament. I have some ideas on how you could have made the Triwizard tasks a lot easier, quicker, and less nerve-racking for you.

First of all, the first task was much easier than you think. You and Mad-Eye Moody both thought of the same way to get the egg. You thought the best way to steal it from the Horntail was to summon your Firebolt from the school and lure the Horntail into the air, away from its nest, so you could take the egg.

Believe it or not, there was a much simpler way to do that. Since you worked extra hard to learn the Summoning charm, why not summon the egg right from under the Horntail's belly? All you had to do was create a diversion, for instance, shoot a few birds from your wand at the Horntail like Mr. Olivander did when testing Victor Krum's wand. When you are completely sure that the Horntail has its full attention on the birds, you summon the egg right into your hand and get the best marks. If you forgot the incantation for the birds, it's "avis."

Now then, on to the second task. I don't think you could have done anything to get ready for the second task. It was very lucky Dobby was so eager to repay you for the Christmas present. I don't think you should have known to ask Neville for info on underwater breathing. Anyway, I think it was very brave of you to try to protect the other hostages, giving up a great score in the meantime.

The third task was the thing you could have changed the most. You see, if you had used an easier way to touch the

Cup first, you could have saved a life. This way is even simpler than the first task, though it also involves the summoning charm. The rules in this task say that the first person to touch the Cup wins, right? But it doesn't say anything about where in the maze you touch the Cup! All you have to do is wait until Cedric is out of sight, then summon the Triwizard Cup right off its pedestal, over the hedges, and into your hand! Not only will you win straightforward, untied, and with two uninjured legs, but then no harm will come to Cedric. You would escape from Lord Voldemort just like you really did and have a lot less guilt and unhappiness for the rest of the year. You'll still have some, though. Those unhappy thoughts will be memories from Voldemort's father's grave, of course.

And so, in conclusion, if you had thought of these things, your year would have been a lot better, with less panic. One other person would be living right now, and you would have been able to enjoy being in a tournament that three people out of seven hundred generations would be able to enjoy.

Sincerely,
Brian

Dear Harry,

Ever since I started reading about your adventures I've admired you an awful lot. I wish I could attend Hogwarts and learn to ride the broom and help you out in Potions class. How does it feel to ride a broom? Isn't it scary to have such a thin stick carrying you so high above? Are you ever afraid you'll fall off? Still, I bet it's wonderful to swerve around blooming trees in the spring and feel the gentle breeze upon your face. You're such a lucky boy.

Are there any ghosts in the boys bathroom? I know there's one in the girls' bathroom. Do you ever wish you had a little brother or sister? I'm an only child, and I get really lonely sometimes. Ron is so fortunate to have so many siblings. It must be fun to visit his house. Can you send me a moving picture of yourself? Do you think it'll be possible for a regular Muggle to see it move? What's your favorite type of candy? Is it Bott's Beans? Is there some sort of witch's college that you will attend after Hogwarts? Anyway, I think that's all for now. I hope you'll write back soon.

Take care,
Veronika
Age 16
Brooklyn, New York

Interview with Veronika

I've always loved reading, but with *Harry Potter,* I love it even more. It's the kind of book that you just can't put down. All my friends who have read the Harry Potter books have read each of them in one or two days, reading well into the night each time. It just has some special magic that kind of glues you to it.

All the magic that takes place seems so real. J. K. Rowling's descriptions are so vivid that one can almost picture oneself being there, and participating in all the events.

One of the things that makes *Harry Potter* so wonderful to read is that he's a good person. He can serve as a role model for younger children. At the same time, the fact that Harry has lost both his parents makes it easier for many readers to identify with him—probably those whose parents are divorced. Besides the serious stuff, it's just so fun. So many exciting and interesting things happen in the books that you could never imagine could happen.

Harry's a great character, of course, but my favorite, I would have to say, is Ron. He's just so fun. He's a great friend, and he's so funny with his red hair and freckles.

If I could use just one magical item from *Harry Potter.* I would definitely want a Nimbus broom (of the latest model, of course). It would be so cool to fly high up in the air, like a dream come true.

I really have no ideas for the series. The books seem so perfect already, I can't think of anything that would improve them!

Dear Harry Potter,

I am your BIGGEST fan!! My name is Suzanne, and I live in England, the Muggle World. I have a few questions that I would like you to answer, please.

I can't wait to buy a broom, but am not sure which one. Can you help? I also want to buy a phoenix, but where can you get them? You might have to ask Dumbledore on that one. . . .

I should be at Hogwarts. I'd be really good there. I'm a fast learner (maybe you could put in a good word for me!).

I must go. Hope the Dursleys treat you well! (Ha!)

From,
Suzanne
England

Dear Harry,

I know that you have had horrible experiences with the Dursleys, but don't let them give you a bad impression of Muggles. Some of us Muggles aren't that bad. If you weren't an underaged wizard, you could use a spell to disable them from touching you so you could do whatever you wanted. You should ask Fred and George for some more Ton-Tongue Toffee for Dudley.

I have read a lot about you. Don't worry, Rita Skeeter didn't write any of it. Hermione has told me a lot about you and how wonderful it is to be able to do magic. Hermione and I have been friends, even before she received her acceptance letter to Hogwarts School of Witchcraft and Wizardry. We met one day in London, and we have kept in touch ever since. I usually go to her house over the summer. Maybe she can introduce us some time.

You should try to ignore Malfoy and his brainless Slytherin friends, Crabbe and Goyle. Malfoy is just jealous of you and,

SYRENA
DONÉ

possibly, your father. Your father earned respect from the community because of his personality, and he died, honorably, fighting against Voldemort to save his family. Mr. Malfoy is a Death Eater, who has to use his money and threaten people to make them listen to him. Malfoy just wants attention-your attention. Snape sounds a little jealous, too. By the way, has your scar hurt lately?

How is Hogwarts? Which class is your favorite? I think I would enjoy Care of Magical Creatures and Herbology the most. Hagrid seems to have a warm heart. You should try not to get into fights with Ron over silly things because he is one of those people who is close to you forever, no matter what. Don't forget that he has six siblings, hand-me-downs, and that he is always in your shadow.

I heard about the Triwizard Tournament from Hermione. She talks about you as if you were a god. That was very generous of you to give Fred and George one thousand galleons. What is it like taking the Hogwarts Express?

Have you heard from Sirius lately? I think it is very important that you two stay in touch. He must really care about you. He came all the way to Hogwarts and revealed himself in front of a worried mother and a couple of teachers, all for your safety. I hope that someday he won't have to hide, and you two can live happily together.

What is it like to push off the ground and soar as high as an eagle on a broom? I think it would feel extraordinary to be able to leave all your problems on the ground while you gracefully fly through the air. I should ask Hermione if she can give me a ride sometime. Is your Firebolt functioning properly? What is it like to play Quidditch? It must be great to be able to go somewhere new, find something you're good at, and stick to it.

Well, I must really ask Hermione to introduce us sometime. Take care of yourself. Always think about the best possibilities, not the worst.

Love,
Meghan
Selden, New York

To: Mr. Harry Potter
Hogwarts School of Witchcraft and Wizardry
Gryffindor Tower Boys Dormitory
Four Poster Bed Number Three

Dear Harry Potter,

I've been wondering, who's your favorite teacher? I suspect not Professor Snape or Quirell, but is your favorite teacher Professor Lupin or Dumbledore?

I have always wondered, are those four-poster beds comfy and warm? Does it drive you crazy how Neville Longbottom snores? I think it would drive me nuts! Who do you like better, Ron or Hermione? I like Ron better. In the Triwizard Tournament, who is your favorite opponent? Vikor Krum, the famous Quidditch seeker for Bulgaria who played in the Quidditch World Cup and is from the Durmstrang School of Witchcraft and Wizardry? Or do you like Fleur Delacour, the drop-dead gorgeous girl from Beauxbatons School of Witchcraft and Wizardry? Or do you like Cedric Diggory, a fellow student of Hogwarts from Hufflepuff House. (My favorite of your opponents was Cedric Diggory.)

I also want to know what your favorite subject in school is. I bet not Potions in the dungeons with Snape. The subject I would like most would be Transfiguration with Professor McGonagall.

Thank you for your time. I find your adventures so fascinating.

Sincerely,
Paul
Age 10
Washington, D.C.

Editor's Note: These letters come from the Palo Verde Elementary School in Tulare, California. Thanks to teacher Kimberly Bishop for passing them along.

Dear Harry,

How did you get in a book? My teacher read the whole book to me. How long did you take to do it? Did you and your friends make the book? Are there really three-headed dogs, because I haven't seen a three-headed dog? I like when somebody got a bad flavor of Every Flavour Beans. Do you have a dog or cat or any animals? I have five sisters and five brothers.

Signed,
Denning
Tulare, California

Dear Harry Potter,

How are you doing today? I am doing fine in Palo Verde School. How is it at Hogwarts? Harry, what has been going on? How are Dudley and Aunt Petunia and Uncle Vernon, too? How old are you? I am 8 years old. How are Hermione and Ron doing, too? Do you know Santa Claus and his reindeer and his elves and his wife, Mrs. Claus? Do Ron and Hermione know them? Mrs. Norris, does she do magic? Does that diary really talk? If it really talks, that is very cool. Does it do magic, too? You know Hagrid. Tell me, is he really a giant? Because if he is, I want to know.

Your friend,
Kristin
Tulare, California

Dear Harry,

Are you really magic? Did Mrs. Norris really get frozen? I liked reading your book. What is it like being a wizard? Do you like Hogwarts? Do you have Study Hall in Hogwarts? What is your favorite animal? Your books are good. Do you know what our solar system looks like? What's your favorite color? Mine is blue. What's your teacher's name? Mine is Miss Bishop. We are making maps of Tulare County. I like all kinds of animals. Do you know the ABC's in Sinlagig? I do. Is Filch sad that his cat is frozen?

My school is nice. I know some teachers but some teachers don't know me. I have all kinds of friends. Some people are funny. I am sometimes funny, too. Fluffy sounds mean but I think he isn't really. My teacher read us the first and second books already.

Your friend,
Varidee
Tulare, California

Dear Harry Potter,

Your book is my favorite. I feel sorry for you because Uncle Vernon is so mean. I couldn't believe it when you crashed the car! I wonder what's going to happen next.

Your friend,
Nestor
Tulare, California

Dear Harry Potter,

Do you know what the monster looks like? Are you sure it's Hagrid's monster? I like your books-I'm on the third one. I heard that your mom and dad died. I know how you feel-my mom had a baby, and it died in her stomach. Everyone is so sad.

Do Ron and Hermione play Quidditch? Did it feel weird to talk to a diary? Do you like being a wizard? If the Dursleys boss you around, why don't you use magic on them? Then they won't boss you around.

For Christmas I want a scooter. What do you want? Do you ever get booger-flavor beans, or throw-up-flavor beans?

Harry Potter, your book is the best in the world. I wish I could make a book like yours.

Your friend,
Katelyn
Tulare, California

Dear Harry,

Harry, how does it feel when you're a wizard? Why don't you like Snape? Do you like anything besides Quidditch? What were you for Halloween? Do you have any pets? How did that book talk to you?

From,
Edgar
Tulare, California

Dear Harry Potter,

What happened to the Dursleys? What happened to your parents? My name is Leticia, and I am reading your first book. I am on the chapter "The Boy Who Lived."

My teachers are Ms. Bishop and Mrs. Martin and Mrs. Gimbarty is my reading teacher. Mrs. Gimbarty is reading your first book, too. And Ms. Bishop has all your books. And Ms. Bishop is reading your second book, but I don't know what happened in the beginning. I know how that potion tasted, and it was cool when you talked to the snake, and I didn't like when Hermione went to the hospital because she had put cat hairs in her potion, and now Ms. Bishop is reading us the fourteenth chapter.

I love all your books.

Love,
Leticia
Tulare, California

Dear Harry,

Are you having a nice time at Hogwarts? I hope you are. What is your favorite potion? Have you learned any tricks? I hope you have. Do you like to do magic? Do you know a lot of magic tricks? Do you like to play Quidditch a lot? I think your friends are really nice. Do you have any more friends where the Dursleys live? I think you don't, because Dudley and his gang are always looking for you to hit you, but somehow you always get away. But now that you know magic, you could do something to Dudley.

From,
Carina
Tulare, California

Dear Harry,

What is it like to be a wizard? I am Muggle-born. Harry, why do you not like Snape? Why do you like Quidditch? Do you live in the United States? Harry, what's your address? I want to be a wizard just like you and know some secrets. What was it like to be in a diary, especially someone else's? Harry, do you have any more friends? I have a lot of friends. Or should I say, I used to. I want to have all of your books. I want to know all of your friends.

Signed,
Devon
Tulare, California

Dear Harry,

Do you know any magic tricks yet? What's your favorite subject? What's your favorite food? Do you like math? Do you like to play Quidditch? What's your favorite holiday? What do you want for Christmas? I want a scooter for Christmas. What teacher is your favorite? How tall are you, Harry? Is Quidditch your favorite sport? Do you like Potions? I like to play soccer and basketball. I like pizza. Do you like pizza, Harry?

Signed,
Ozzie (Osbaldo)
Tulare, California

Dear Harry Potter,

Who stole the diary? Do you like Hogwarts? If I went there, it would be fun. Do you have a brother or sister? What's your mom's name? What's your dad's name? What's your age? Mine is 8, and my sister is 11, and my little sister is 2 years old. And do you have a pet? I do. My pet is a snake. And do you have a bike? I do. It is called the Hot Rod. What is yours called if you have one? And where do you live? I live in Tulare with my mom and dad and my sister Beth and my other sister Hannah.

Signed,
Corey
Tulare, California

Dear Harry,

How have you been? I hope you get my letter. Why don't you write me back? I know you are trying to get back to Hogwarts. I know it's hard, just like my school. Tell Ron and Hermione "hi." I never told you my name. My name is Desiree. What's happening? My teacher told the class that there is a big problem, something's going to happen to one of you, but she won't tell us which one. We have to wait for tomorrow. I don't want to wait for tomorrow. Everybody wanted her to read the next part. Is your schoolwork hard? My work is very, very hard. You are lucky that you are in a higher grade than me. Do you wish your parents could be with you right now? It's almost recess now. You're lucky you get to go outside all the time. I hope you have a Merry Christmas.

Your friend,
Desiree
Tulare, California

Dear Harry,

Harry, my name is Javier. Do you like going to Hogwarts? I like to go to school. It is fun to go to school. I like it because you get to play at recess. I like to go to recess and play basketball all recess. Do you like to play in your recess? What are your favorite games to play at recess? Do you like the slide or soccer, basketball or football? I wish I could go to Hogwarts.

Signed,
Javier
Tulare, California

To: Harry Potter
Dear Harry,

I like your stories. What will happen to the diary? Do you like to play basketball? Is your book real? Is your school real? Do you have lots of friends to play with you? Do they play with you on the playground? What's going to happen to you and to Ron or Hermione?

From,
Frankie
Tulare, California

Dear Harry,

I am a Muggle. I think that I really like one of your best friends, Hermione. I admire your courage, the way u faced Voldemort . . . oops, sorry, the way u faced You-Know-Who. I'm already 10 years old.

Hope I see u in Hogwarts.

Sincerely yours,
Steffanie
Singapore

Dear Harry,

I can't imagine what it would be like to be you or your friends. I would trade lives any day even if Voldemort is trying to kill you. If I could have one wish come true, it would be that you were real, Hogwarts and all magical places and people were real. I want to be Hermione, even though she is a know-it-all!

If I was headmaster, the first thing I would do would be to fire Snape, just for you!

I have started writing my own book, and it is called *Harry Potter and the Godfather*. It's about you getting a girlfriend named Rosie Pottary, and her parents and sister died like yours! If you are thinking it was Voldemort, you're wrong. In my book, it's Snape. He's after you, but don't worry-you could never die. You're the main character! Your godfather saves you, and the Ministry catches him, puts the Truth-Telling spell on him, and he tells what really happened when the crime occurred. So his name is cleared and you get to live with him!!! How cool. No more Harry-hunting for Dudley!! No more staying with Mrs. Figg even though she is a witch. Well, I hope to get it published someday.

What is your favorite class? Mine would be Charms or Defense Against the Dark Arts!

Love,
Ciera
Age 14
Lamoni, Iowa

Interview with Ciera

Ciera tells me that before the Harry Potter books came out, she never liked to read. But now she does. She credits her friend Heather, who first told her about *Harry Potter.* Here's what happened next: "So I got the books and couldn't put them down until I was done!"

"Cool adventures" are what Ciera likes most about the Harry Potter books. "Like when he found the mirror of Erised. It made me cry when he saw his parents and the rest of the Potter family. Also, I liked the dangerous events in Book Four."

Her favorite characters (after Harry, of course) are Hermione and Ron. "I like them because the they stick up for each other and don't do anything dangerous without the other two."

"The magical item I would like to have from *Harry Potter* would definitely be a Firebolt. I would love to fly in the air . . . and play Quidditch!!

"What I'm hoping to find out from future books is more about Harry's parents."

Dear Harry,

How are you? I hope the Dursleys are at least treating you better than before. I wish Draco would get expelled-he makes me really mad. I would love to go to Hogwarts but unfortunately I don't. How's Quidditch coming? It's my favorite sport, and I hope Gryffindor is winning. I can't wait to hear about your next adventure. *Kushti bok!* or, "Good luck with your classes!"

Walk on,
Cherry
age 13
Clinton Township, Michigan

Here is my little sister's letter to Hagrid.

Dear Hagrid,

I think you are great! How does it feel to know Harry Potter? I would like to have a boar hound like Fang, even if he is a coward. Is there a way where I could meet you sometime?

Cheers,
Axis
age 10
Clinton Township, Michigan

Dear Harry,

How can you put up with Professor Snape? It's not fair that he gives just the Gryffindors points off! That's really mean!

I like Hagrid. He tried so hard to make his lesson on Magical Creatures so good. Of course, Malfoy had to ruin it! I bet Malfoy meant to! Malfoy's horrible!

So how's Quidditch? It sounds like a really fun game! Well, any game would be fun if you're allowed to fly on broomsticks!

I think in your fifth year you should stay undercover. With You-Know-Who around, it will be a very exciting year! Watch out, Harry. He might be behind any door!

From your fan,
Kristy
Maine

Dear Harry Potter,

Hello. My name is Katie, and I love reading about you, your friends, and, your adventures. I would like to congratulate you on winning the Triwizard Tournament. You were great! What's it like at Hogwarts?Is it fun? Please tell Hermione and Ron I said hello and wish them good luck next year at Hogwarts. I hope the Dursleys, Slytherins, and Snape are treating you okay. Not to worry, because with your fans, friends, and godfather on your side cheering you on, you will be able to accomplish anything you set your mind on. Please write back.

With love from your number one fan,
Katie
South Australia

Dear Harry,

You are definitely my favorite hero! Why do you think you are always in the middle of trouble? What is it like for you to have half the girls in the school in love with you? If I were you, I'd consider it an honor. Harry, you are so lucky. You always have the best of everything. I'm sorry. Do I sound a bit Malfoyish? I'm writing this while listening to *Harry Potter* and the *Chamber of Secrets,* the chapter "The Rogue Bludger." It must be wonderful to be up in the air on a broomstick. I think if I was a witch I would like to be a beater. Is Dudley really fatter than he is tall? Ouch! That's fat!

Your biggest fan in Oregon,
Julia

Dear Harry,

You probably don't know me. My name is Clare. I am from Beauxbatons, and last year when my best friend's sister came back, she told us how you bravely saved her from the Merpeople.

Well, to get to the point, my English teacher said that we had to choose someone to be our pen pal so we could practice English. We had to pull names out of a hat, and I got you.

So I went to the library to look for books about you. But I wanted to know the truth. Do you really have a crush on Hermione or are you just faking it? Well, it's time to go.

From,
Clare

P.S. My English teacher wrote this in English for you.

Dear Harry,

Question-Harry Potter, do you plan on becoming a school Prefect? I love *Harry Potter*. Your books are awesome! I love them! I can't wait till number five (book)!!!

HARRY POTTER ROCKS!!!

Katie
Rickreall, Oregon

Dear Harry,

How is Hog? I would love to go to THAT place but you know . . .

How is Hagrid doing? And Hermione? I love your friend Ron-he is so funny. Is your scar annoying?

I would like to meet you somehow someday.

Bye for now.

Love,
Olivia
Sydney, N.S.W
Australia

Mr. H. Potter
The Cupboard Under the Stairs
Privet Drive
Little Whinging
Surrey

To My Dearest Harry,

How are you? Is Dudley still annoying you? I certainly hope not! How are Hermione and Ron? Say hello to them when you see them next, please. I'm sorry I didn't send this letter by owl post, but last week my owl died so I'll have to get another one. Speaking of which, how's Hedwig? I hope she's all right. If Dudley keeps annoying you, try this spell: HOCUS-POCUS, VOODOO HOODOO, DO THE THINGS I TELL YOU TO DO! It's a very good spell, and you should also use it on Malfoy and Snape. I hate Snape-he has to be the worst teacher alive! How is Hagrid? I haven't seen him for a long time. How's Quidditch? I'm really good at it. I'm thinking about joining the team! I'm going to see Hermione tomorrow. Do you want to come? If you do, meet me at Zonko's Joke Shop and then we'll leave for Hermione's, but don't forget to bring money so we can buy some things and we can go to Honeydukes!

I have to leave now and do my Defense Against the Dark Arts project. Sorry!

I'll see you tomorrow.

Yours sincerely,
Rosie
(Your DEAREST Friend)
Victoria
Australia

Dear Harry,

Can you make us a robot witch that's gonna clean up the laundry room and the toy room, and it can fly?

We have a riding stick with a horse head on it that makes a galloping noise when you pinch her ear. Can you give us some tips on how to make it fly?

From,
Sarah and Jeremy
Ages 7 and 5
Potomac, Maryland

Hi, Harry,

How are you doing? I hope you are good and that Malfoy isn't annoying you too much. I don't think I would be able to stand him for more then a day, or Snape for that matter.

I hope Snape isn't being too mean to you. And I hope you stand up for Neville because it's not his fault that he is a forgetful, clumsy boy. I mean everybody is clumsy at one stage of their life. But maybe not as much as Neville.

What about Professor Trelawny? I hope she isn't predicting your death anymore. I don't think I could stand it if she was doing that to me. I'd throw my crystal ball at her head. Okay, maybe I wouldn't go that far!

Are you ready for the next Quidditch match? Who are you against this time? Whoever it is, there's no way they'll beat you. You're too good. The whole team is.

Tell Hagrid that I agree with him about all the dangerous creatures. They are cute. I don't know what anybody has against them.

Well, I should go.

Bye,
From,
Ashleigh
Age 12
Melbourne, Australia

Interview with Ashleigh

Ashleigh has long been a good reader but her enthusiasm grew even greater when the Harry Potter books came on the scene. She says: "I've always enjoyed reading. There was never a time when I wasn't reading some sort of book in my free time. But when I was introduced to *Harry Potter,* my liking for books did grow. I'm not exactly sure why but I started reading any and every book that looked like it had something to do with magic."

I asked what made the Harry Potter books different from others she'd read and enjoyed, and she replied, "That is a really hard question to answer. Heaps of people have asked me but you can't answer it. *Harry Potter* is the best book I have ever read but you can't pinpoint what you like about it. Or you just can't put it into words. I suppose one reason I like it so much is because of the way it is written. The way it makes you believe things that turn out to be very wrong in the end, the way evil people turn out to be the good ones and good ones become evil. The way you have to read the book again to pick up the little bits you missed last time. These are only a few reasons, but if I was to tell you all the reasons it would take forever."

I next asked which character she liked most (not counting Harry, of course). Ashleigh had no trouble with that one, which she said, "is simple to answer. Fred and George Weasley. I think I like them so much because I used be like that. I don't do it anymore (which sucks) but I used to pull pranks all the time. I love the chapters with them in it because you can't help laughing. I hope they still stay in the book somehow after they leave Hogwarts. It just wouldn't be the same without them."

Ashleigh, like so many of the kids I talked to, would take a flying broomstick, if she could have just one magical item from the book. And what would she use it for? To play Quidditch, of course! But beyond its use for the sport, she adds, "The thought of being able to hop on a broom and being able to fly away from everything, interests me."

The idea of a mere child having such power strikes Ashleigh as one of the main appealing features of the book for kids. She explains, "You read books and watch movies about adults who become superheroes and save the world. I think that kids like Harry Potter because it's someone closer to their own age saving the day. It's easier for them to understand Harry in some parts. There's also the fact that he has lost his parents and a lot of kids start to feel sorry for him. There's at least one stage when a kid wishes that they didn't have parents and that they could do what they liked. But when they read about Harry growing up in the cupboard under the stairs and living with his horrible aunt and uncle, they don't mind having their own parents. I think that the reason that adults like the book is because it's been a long time since they were able to imagine magic and fairies. *Harry Potter* was introduced to me by a man over forty with five children and a wife. He also happened to be my grade six teacher. He absolutely loved the book. Adults sometimes forget what it's like to be a kid."

As for the direction that the books may take later on, Ashleigh does worry a bit that Ms. Rowling may let herself be influenced by what her fans suggest. Ashleigh urges her to trust her own vision, instead: "I don't think anybody should start telling or suggesting anything about the books to J. K. Rowling. I think they are going perfectly fine. Just so long as she keeps writing for herself and not anybody else. You sometimes see writers or bands turn bad because they start to get a lot of money. I hope that doesn't happen to our favorite author, and I doubt it will. I hope that the books stay the way they are now—absolutely wonderful."

Dear Harry,

When's your next book coming out? How's Hedwig? Doing any better in Quidditch?

How about Ron–is he over his broken leg?

Bother Dudley for me.

Sincerely,
Marissa

Dear Harry Potter,

My friend Taylor is acting like he is a wizard, and I've been playing along. If you are real or if you get this note, come to my house and turn me into a witch with an owl. I told Taylor I've got an owl and a hippogiff with babies, and its name is Kiwi and my dog is named Sochie and she has puppies, too, and I said that Voldemort is my uncle and Black was my guardian and that we were brothers and sisters and I'm serious about that spell. See ya in my house when you turn me into a witch. Turn Dudley into a big glob of mud, and I will see you this summer and I don't want to tell you what I got you for Christmas.

Your fake sister and fake witch,
Kelsea
age 9
El Paso, Arkansas

P.S. I love you! Come secretly because I live with Voldemort.

Interview with Kelsea

Has Harry Potter *changed your attitude toward reading and books at all?*

Yes! It's made me enjoy reading even more because I love Harry, and my friend and I play like we are witches and wizards. And I told him that Harry was my brother!

What do you like most about Harry Potter?

What I like most about *Harry Potter* is that Harry is a wizard, and I like witches and wizards, and I just love magic. I'd train as hard as I could if I could go to witch school.

Aside from Harry, who's your favorite character?

My second favorite character is Hagrid because I like magical creatures a lot, just like he does.

If you could use one spell or magical item from Harry Potter, *which one would you pick?*
If I could use one magical item, I would buy a Firebolt and fly it!

Why do you think Harry Potter *has been such a huge success with kids?*
I think that they love to read it because it gives kids and even grown-ups a chance to relax and believe.

Do you have any ideas or suggestions of your own for J. K. Rowling to use in her next book?
J. K. Rowling, I have an idea for you: Make a book about Hagrid and Harry when he's got a job. I think Harry and Hermione will get romantic, and they'll get married and have a family.

Dear Harry,

It's too bad Professor McGonagall doesn't favor the Gryffindors but at least she hates the Slytherins. You should think up a plot to get Malfoy suspended or even better, expelled. Actually, I have a plan for you: I don't know what spell you would need but if you told Malfoy to meet you in a room in the middle of the night, he would take his chance to get at you. You would go, but in the Invisibility Cloak. When you got there you would cast a spell for him to do evil things. Then lock him in. Oh, I forgot, before you do that, at about five o'clock, tip Filch off about Malfoy. Then go a bit earlier than the time you told Filch. When Filch gets there Malfoy would be casting evil spells in the middle of the night when he was supposed to be in bed. Maybe Filch would even reward you for telling him about Malfoy.

What do you think?

From,
Erin
Age 9
Nevada City, California

Interview with Erin

Nine-year-old Erin from California has already zipped through all four Harry Potter books and now is impatiently awaiting the fifth. "I was so excited about the fourth one," she told me, "that I couldn't stop reading it. I was mad at myself for finishing it so quickly because I wanted to have a lot of time to enjoy it!"

Harry may be a boy wizard from England, but Erin has no trouble identifying with him. "He has some of the same qualities as me. He is adventuresome and brave—both qualities that I have and admire. Just from reading the first book, you already have a picture inside your brain. To me the number one thing about him could easily be that he is willing to risk his life for his friends."

Erin's second favorite character is (no surprise here) Hermione. Erin says, "She is a finicky pickle but she is loyal and kind. At the beginning of the series she was a brat and a show-off but she felt very warm toward Harry and Ron for saving her, so she became their friends."

I asked Erin if she wished she could have any of Harry's magic things or use any of his spells, and Erin, instead of choosing to fly on a broomstick or sneak around under an Invisibility Cloak and make mischief (as so many other children wished to do) instead quickly responded: "I would chose a spell to heal my friends. I would not chose a spell to hurt my enemy. If possible, I would try not to be nasty to my enemy."

Next I asked Erin what she thought set the Harry Potter books apart from other books for kids. At first she started to talk about Harry's adventures but when I ventured the thought that lots of kids' books are adventure stories, she added, "Harry Potter books are so great because of the ideas that J. K. Rowling came up with and also the way she puts things. She has a brilliant mind full of interesting words."

As for my call for suggestions for Ms. Rowling to use in future Harry Potter books, Erin respectfully declined. "I think she is so talented that I can't think of a single thing to suggest to make her writing better."

Dear Harry,

I am Joshua. I live in Costa Rica but I am from Canada. I discovered the stories about you from my friend Zak. He had the first book, and he lent it to me, and I immediately loved the book. When he told me there was a second and third, I bought them right away. When I finished reading them I couldn't wait until the fourth came out. I already read it and that has been the best for me. I cannot wait until the fifth book and the movie come out. I think the stories are better than the rumors. I hope they come out very soon.

Joshua
Age 10
San Jose, Costa Rica

Interview with Joshua

Joshua isn't one of those kids who was hooked on *Harry Potter* from day one. Instead, he admits, "When I started reading *Harry Potter*, it seemed very boring. But I kept on reading . . . and it was so cool. I learned that you should keep on reading a book even if it seems boring at first."

What ultimately won him over is Harry's perseverance. Harry's life seemed kind of pathetic to Joshua at the start of the book, but he soon discovered that Harry was more than a match for his awful circumstances. "The thing I like most about Harry Potter is he is a boy who never gives up. He fights the unbeatable, and he wins."

But Joshua is fascinated by some of the darker characters as well. When I asked him which character he liked best, after Harry, he told me: "Snape, because there is so much to find out about him."

Joshua's got a mischievous streak in him, which affects his choice for the one magical item from the book he wishes he could use: "The Invisibility Cloak, because you can sneak out and fool people."

Joshua isn't shy about giving J. K. Rowling advice about the direction of future books. Here's one plot twist he suggests: "For once she should make the guy who seems the bad guy really *be* the bad guy." Here's something else he'd like to see: a new character, an exchange student from a wizard school in Brazil. I doubt very much if J. K. Rowling has thought of that one!

Hi, Harry,

How are things with Voldemort? It would be weird going to school every year, knowing in one way or another, he was going to try and kill you again, and you have to defeat him again. All in a day's work, though, huh? I don't know why you stick with Divination. If Trelawney predicts your death again, throw a crystal ball at her head. Or better still, save the ball for Snape. D'you think in the future, Muggles and magical people would play Quidditch together? Then maybe we could teach you Aussie Rules football. We'll see how it goes. Tell Ron and Hermione I said hi, from someone who wishes they were magical.

Alex
Melbourne, Australia

The following letters are from Verstovia Elementary School in Sitka, Arkansas.

Hi, Harry,

How's life? Is that mangy cat, Mrs. Norris, still wandering around? Is your homework getting any funner? I wonder where Voldemort will turn up next? I hope he doesn't turn up anywhere.

Sincerely,
Your fellow wizard,
Caitlin

Dear Harry Potter,

I think I would like to go to Hogwarts. But I would hate Potions lessons. I think that Snape is very, very, very unfair to you and your fellow Gryffindors.

I have a question: Why does Voldemort want to kill you so bad? Before you got your scar, you were just an ordinary 1-year-old-boy. If you know the answer, please send me a letter (by return owl).

Yours truly,
Kari

Hello, Harry,

Why do Ron and Hermione fight so much? I mean, she helps you with your homework and stuff, so why do they fight?

Also, I think your books are really great! It's neat that you get to "get" Malfoy, if you know what I mean. Is Snape still bugging you? I hope Professor McGonagall isn't giving you too much homework. Did Ron get the niffler he wanted? Anyway, I have to go.

Berret
Order of Merlin, First Class
Extreme Sorceress

Dear Harry Potter,

How are Sirius and Buckbeak? Do you really think He Who Must Not Be Named is going to kill you? It was very nice of Dobby to get that gillyweed to you. I think it was good that you got Fleur's sister from the lake; she was very glad.

Your friend,
Abigail

Dear Harry,

Hi. My name is Taylor, and I'm one of your biggest fans! I'd love to visit Hogwarts someday. By the sound of it, I think it would be great to go to a school like that. Although it would be much better without Snape and Malfoy. If I was at Hogwarts now I'd probably love it! But unfortunately I'm just a normal Muggle who's way into magic and Hogwarts. I really wish I could be at Hogwarts right now. Well, anyway, there's not much of a chance I'll be picked, but I'll remain one of your biggest fans. One last thing, I was wondering about Quidditch so I was hoping you could send a letter back about Quidditch.

Sincerely,
Taylor

Dear Harry Potter,

Is it fun knowing how to do magic? I wish I could do magic. If I did, I would cast a spell on my sister to make her stop bugging me. It must be exciting to go to Hogwarts. I would like to. What is your favorite class? I think mine would be Charms. How can you play Quidditch so well? Do you like going on exciting adventures? Most of them sound scary.

I would like to be like you. It sounds fun. I read all your books.

Your friend,
Nickelle

Dear Harry,

I love to read your books. I have no clue how you can take on Malfoy! When will Book Five come out? What was it like when you were flying in the car? What are Hagrid's cakes like-I bet rocks. I'm glad I don't find barf beans in Every Flavor Beans. I think you're the very, very most extremely best! I can't wait till You-Know-Who is dead! Were you surprised when Hermione kissed you?

Your biggest fan,
Erika

Hi, Harry,

I love your books. You are the best. What is it like on a broomstick?

Your pal,
Dylan
Lilydale, Australia

Interview with Dylan

Dylan loves *Harry Potter* because he loves "reading about the characters doing magic and other things that normal people can't do." He particularly loves Hermione, not so much for any qualities in her character, but "because she has a very smart cat." His third favorite character is Dumbledore "because he's funny."

If Dylan could *be* Harry Potter, what he thinks he'd like best is owning a flying broomstick. "It would be the best fun flying it!" he says, with no fear at all about falling off.

But he thinks a large part of the appeal of the series lies in the villainy of Voldemort. "He's such a scary character, and even though Harry always gets away, you still are afraid that he might not, so you have to read more to find out what happens."

Dear Harry Potter,

Hi! I'm Kina. I think that Snape is too harsh. Why is the scar on your head in the shape of a lightning bolt? Our class is reading *Harry Potter and the Sorcerer's Stone.* I've read the first book about six times. This is my second time reading the second book. I think that second one is the coolest. My friend and I came up with turning our school into Hogwarts. The four fourth grade classes are Hufflepuff, Ravenclaw, Gryffindor, and Slytherin. Mr. Geier's class (my class) is Gryffindor, Mrs. Olson's is Hufflepuff, Mrs. Sander's is Ravenclaw, and Mr. Peper is Slytherin (he's sort of like Snape). Art is astronomy, music class is Herbology, P.E. is Defense against the Dark Ages, Science is Care of Magical Creatures, G.A.T.E is Divination. We're still thinking up the rest.

Your BIGGEST FAN,
Cristina Elizabeth (or Kina
Butter Jelly)
Henderson, Nevada

Leah, Kina's partner in the move to transform the fourth grade into Hogwarts continues with her own account of events:

Dear Harry Potter,

Hi! Who is your favorite teacher at Hogwarts? (Professor Dumbledore is not included.) Mine is either Professor Lupin or Professor McGonagal. My friend and I came up with an idea to turn our school, Estes McDaniel, into Hogwarts. Since we are in fourth grade, we made the four fourth grade classes the houses. My teacher is Mr. Geier. We (my friend and I) made Mr. Geier's class Gryffindor. He is really funny. We made Mrs. Olson's class Hufflepuff, Mrs. Sander's is Ravenclaw, and Mr. Peper's class is Slytherin. We thought he might be suitable as Snape. (No offense toward him.) We made special classes be things like Herbology and Divination. We made the lunchroom the main hall. Anyways, we still need the principal's permission. Well, gotta go! Bye!

Your number one fan,
Leah
Henderson, Nevada

P.S. I've read all four of your books!

Dear Harry Potter,

I thought of two new curses you might like.

1. This charm is good to use in a battle:

PUKAWIZZYATYA

It means: to make hockey pucks fly.

2. This charm can only be used on Draco Malfoy.

BAKO BAKO DRACO

It means: to make him hot!

From your friend,
Joey
Age 7
Nesconset, New York

Interview with Joey

Reading *Harry Potter* has made me enjoy reading more because they are LONG books, and my mom and dad read them to me. It is nice to spend time with my parents reading in their room at night.

I like reading *Harry Potter* so much because it is an adventure and a mystery at the same time. I like getting the clues and then finding out the facts at the end.

The thing I like most about Harry is his scar. Everybody is different in this world. It makes Harry stand out as "different" but in a good way. He is strong and has made it through a lot in his life.

My second favorite character is Ron, because he is Harry's best friend. I feel like I know him the best and that he is somebody I would want to be friends with, too.

If I could use one item of Harry's, it would be his Firebolt. I would love to have a broomstick to fly around on. I would be able to go anywhere I wanted without having to ask a grown-up to take me.

My favorite class at Hogwarts is Care of Magical Creatures. That's because I love animals, especially dogs, and I know I would learn love to learn about all of the animals in the wizarding world. I also think Hagrid would be an awesome teacher! I think he is great!

I have an idea for J. K. Rowling for the next book. I think Fred and George should open a joke shop in Hogsmead and call it Wacky Weasley's Wizarding Wonders. They could buy the building with the money Harry gave them and then Sirius and Harry could live in the apartment upstairs during the summers off from the school.

Hi, Harry,

I'm a real wizard, and I would send this letter by owl but this Muggle contraption seemed, well, okay and it's my fifth year at Hogwarts, and I'm your number one fan and well, it's pretty cool talking to you.

Your number one fan,
Brandon

Dear Harry,

So how is it at Hogwarts? How are Ron and Hermione doing? What is your favorite class? Snape is kinda mean. Professor Trelawney is far out! And Mad-Eye Moody is creepy! Lupin was my favorite, favorite Defense against the Dark Arts teacher, too. Is the homework hard at Hogwarts? How was it fighting the Hungarian Horntail? Was it hard? Who is your favorite teacher now, out of Mad-Eye Moody, Hagrid, Professor Trelawney, or Professor McGonagall? Owl me as soon as you can.

Your friend,
A. J.

Dear Harry Potter,

How's life at Hogwarts? Do all the first-years admire you because you are so famous? I sleep in a room that is about the size of your closet at the Dursleys', but my mom is a lot nicer than the Dursleys. But I have a problem with my sister. Can you teach me a spell to keep her out of my room? I really wish I could ride a broom and play Quidditch. If you could do a spell to turn Snape into anything in the world, what would it be? I'd choose a worm since he couldn't bother me if he was a worm. But I definitely wouldn't choose a dragon.

Sincerely,
Jackson
Age 9
Washington, D.C.

Interview with Jackson

The Harry Potter books certainly made a difference in Jackson's attitude toward reading. He says he was amazed that the first one was actually "fun to read, and it made me think how fun other things were to read. Before that, I didn't really like reading all that much."

Being a sports fan, what Jackson admires most about Harry is his skill at Quidditch. But he also likes Ron a lot, "because he's funny. He's the one who says all the funny stuff. I like Fred and George, too."

When I asked him if he thought he could explain Harry Potter's huge appeal to kids, he responded thoughtfully, "I think it's because Harry is a little the same as regular kids . . . but also a little bit different. He has a lot of the same things he thinks about and worries about as regular kids. But he is also magical and that lets my imagination run wild."

As to what Jackson would like to see in future books in the series, he is quite definite: "No romance! More Quidditch! Maybe a new Quidditch team captain." Got that, Ms. Rowling?

Dear Harry,

How are you? What about Hermione and Ron? How are the things going at Hogwarts? Well, I think I'd better introduce myself. My name is Juliana, and I'm 14 years old. I'm wondering if you could find some spells for me so that I can't forget things quickly. I'm absentminded, you know. Does Hermione know any spells that will work? She's really amazing. She's very clever, and one thing's for sure, she's not absent-minded!

Yours,
Juliana
North Sumatra, Indonesia

Dear Harry Potter,

My name is Taylor. I am a fourth-grade student in Mrs. Menke's class. My hobbies are soccer, volleyball, and basketball.

Harry Potter, your books are so interesting. I love reading books like that. I have read all four of your books. They are really great! I really enjoyed number One and Number

Four. Number One tells a lot about Harry. Number Four was just a really good mystery.

Well, Harry, I just hope you like this letter.

Your friend,
Taylor
Gaylord, Michigan

Dear Harry,

I think that you're the best and most powerful wizard I have ever read about. Hogwarts seems like a really neat school. I wish I could go there. You are so lucky to be able to go to a school where you learn magic. What's it like to ride a broomstick? It sounds like a lot of fun. If I were you, I'd do stunts with the broomstick and fly everywhere. How many spells do you know? Do you have a spell that can clean up my room? Let me know. What is your favorite subject at Hogwarts? Mine would be Chemistry.

Do you like to play Quidditch? I think it would be great to play. What's it like to be a seeker on the Quidditch team? I wish I could be on your team. What's it like to play with Oliver Wood?

What was it like to ride the Hogwarts Express? Did you like the food on the train? I would have liked to have seen the movable cards. That would have been really cool.

I don't know of anyone with a pet owl. It must be fun!

It would be great to send letters that way. I hope you get this letter by mail.

Your friend,
David
Age 12
Edmonton, Alberta, Canada

Dear Harry,

How is Hogwarts? Do you like all your teachers? What are your thoughts about Snape, your Potions teacher? Did you like the train ride there? How were the jellies you tried? It would be fun to guess which one you're about to try.

Did you like your first day at school? How did you feel when you got picked to go to Gryffindor's dorm instead of Snape's dorm? Were you scared when you went up to the big sorting hat and when you sang the Hogwarts song? I would have been petrified.

Harry, was it fun to learn to fly on a broomstick? If I were you I'd ride it all day and night. What was it like to play your first Quidditch game? That must have been fun to play a game on your broomstick. Was it fun to be invisible? That would be the best magic trick ever.

It must have been exciting to talk to a picture on the wall and then walk through the wall. I would like to have done that! Harry, how did you feel when you went to a bookstore and you realized that everyone wanted your autograph? How exciting! What was it like when you went to the bank where your mom and dad left you some money? Were you sad?

You have such an adventurous life. I wish I could join you. Best of all, I wish I had a pet owl like you. That would be fun. What an exciting experience!

Sincerely,
Stacey
Age 12
Edmonton, Alberta, Canada

Dear Harry.

G'day. My name is Alexandra, and I'm from Australia. How are things at Hogwarts? I hope Voldermort isn't planning to show up this year-when are you going to get time to study with him around? Only kidding. (Hermione would say something like that.)

Do you know that in Australia, we have our own school of magic? It's called MAGICS (Magical Academy Generalizing In Constructive Spells). I'm only a Muggle, but me and some other kids get to go and talk to the witches and wizards the same age as us and teach them about muggles.

Is Gryffindor leading in the house cup? I hope the Quidditch matches are going well. Just as long as Slytherin remains beaten, it's okay. One thing that bothered me was the suggestion that Malfoy makes a better ferret than he does human. But that's an insult to ferrets! Maybe someone should make a separate school for Slytherins.

I have a spell to help you when Malfoy's really trying to turn you insane. Even if you're not meant to use magic in between classes, this spell is definitely worth a detention: Just say: "Wandious Nummens!" and Malfoy's wand will be frozen numb. Even if he tried to put a curse on you, it wouldn't work because his wand would be numbed. Mind you, it does wear off after a while, so just make sure that you're not within 100 metres of him when his wand works again.

Well, I have to go, but tell everyone at Hogwarts I said G'day.

From a Muggle supporting
magical people,
Alexandra
Age 12
Melbourne, Australia

Interview with Alexandra

I have always enjoyed reading, but never before had I finished reading a 636-page book in two days! It's impossible to put *Harry Potter* down unless you've finished reading the whole thing and you've finally learned what happens.

The thing I like most about *Harry Potter* is the fact that something so impossible, like magic, becomes so real. You can dream about riding a broomstick, knowing that you never can, and then read about this boy who not only rides a broomstick, but plays Quidditch on one. Everything impossible is real and happening before your eyes.

Besides Harry, my favorite characters are Ron and Hermione, because they're so different from each other. They used to hate each other, but somehow turned out best friends. Then my next favorite characters would be Fred and George. Even the teachers think they're funny (most of the time, anyway . . .)!

I think children like reading about Harry Potter so much because he's almost everything they would want to be like. He's a famous hero, he rides a broomstick, he can perform magic, and he's still very young. But even if he is a wizard, they can relate to him, because, like most kids dread math class, he dreads Divination. He isn't good at everything but still gets good grades. He has friends and enemies, and he has his bad days. So he's pretty much human, like all of us.

Though you haven't asked me about this, I just want to bring up the big deal some Christians are making about *Harry Potter* being evil. It's only a book! It's not as if Harry is real and going to come and get you in your sleep. I'm a Christian, and I love *Harry Potter*!

Dear Harry,

I love your adventures. I just can't see how you can deal with not having any parents. When you saw the echoes of your mom and dad, I cried. I am just a big baby like that.

Well, I have conjured up a spell that you can put on your enemy, stupid little brat Draco Malfoy (yucky). Here it is:

Bubble bubble toil and trouble
Time to stop Malfoy's trouble
Now turn Malfoy into a bubble
And we'll stop Malfoy's nasty trouble

I think it may be a good spell. What it does, as you know, is it turns Malfoy into a bubble. I don't know if it would be good to turn Malfoy into a bubble, but hey, you never know.

Well, anyway, I think it would be really cool to be like you. Besides the fact that Voldemort is chasing after you all the time. Oh, and I shouldn't forget the worst of all, the dumb dodo Dursleys. They are the worst! I wish I could be there and teach Dudley a thing or two about being beat up. I may be a girl but I know karate. Well, I hope everything works out for you. Also, that you don't get kicked out of Hogwarts or (dare I say it) get killed. Hope you have a great time!

Best wishes,
Kassandra

Dear Harry.

How's stuff with Malfoy? I hope that Gryffindor is beating Slytherin. I'm not old enough to play Quidditch yet, because I'm only 8, but I really want to. Have you been practicing your Quidditch? I heard that the finals are coming up soon. I wish that I could be you. It would be a fantastic life being a wizard, apart from Voldemort trying to kill you all the time! Do you like being famous? I'm one of your biggest fans.

From a boy who wants to be a wizard,
Dylan
Age 8
Melbourne, Australia

Dear Harry Potter,

There are three things that you get to do that I want to do very badly: I desperately want to fly a broom. I want to do this because I love to ride roller coasters, and I think that it would be a lot like that! I also want to go to Hogwarts. If I could, I would be in Gryffindor. My third and final wish is to have a magic wand. Oh, by the way, could you tell Dumbledore that I would make a great wizard, and am nearly at the age to be accepted at Hogwarts?

From,
Madelaine
Winnetka, Illinois

Dear Harry Potter,

It must be cool being a wizard! I'm really glad you made friends at Hogwarts. Flying a broomstick has been a lifelong dream of mine. Do you think you could send me one by next owl post? I could repay you with my undying admiration. (If that's not enough, just send me a bill!) Good luck in school.

Sincerely,
Matthew
Age 11
Winnetka, Illinois

Dear Harry,

Congratulations on winning the Triwizard Cup! How do you like going to school at Hogwarts? Do you like learning magic instead of math, writing, science, etc.? I wish I could go to Hogwarts. How is Sirius doing? I hope better than he was doing during your fourth year at Hogwarts. Do you think the real Moody is going to be teaching Defense Against the Dark Arts next year, or does Snape want the job?

Are the Dursleys treating you any better? I hope so! If they aren't, I think you should escape to Ron's house for the summer. You should ask him to send you some floo powder by owl, then leave. Has Dudley found any more Ton-Tongue Toffee? If so, how did they get his tongue back to normal size this time?

I'm glad that you won (once again) your battle against Voldemort. I can't wait to hear about your next adventure!

Sincerely,
Leslie
Age 11
Winnetka, Illinois

Dear Harry,

You probably hear this a lot, but I am a huge fan of yours. I love your stories. They are really exciting; I wish I had that many adventures in my life. How's Hogwarts? Does Hermione still have Rita Skeeter? I think you should put the Imperius curse on her. Then you can make her write horrid things about Malfoy and the rest of his stupid followers.

How's Dudley? Maybe you can make a potion to make him explode-it's going to happen to him anyway! Except that might make you have more problems with your aunt and uncle, but if you can handle He-Who-Must-Not-Be-Named, you can definitely handle them. Send me an owl if you need a hand with any potions-I am a whiz at them.

From,
Meghan, Expert Potions Master
Winnetka, Illinois

P.S. Sorry I couldn't send this by owl.

Dear Mr. Potter,

How do you like Hogwarts School?

Were you scared when you met Voldemort? Were you surprised when you found out who was the mean guy with Voldemort?

I wish I had that invisible cloak that you have.

I hope you have fun at your next year at Hogwarts.

Sincerely,
Claire
Age 7
Washington, D.C.

Interview with Claire

Claire had just turned 7 when her mother read her the first Harry Potter book. She hasn't had any of the others read to her yet, because she's waiting until she's old enough to read them on her own. She figures that will be at the beginning of third grade (she's in second grade now). She's already a good reader and has read several Roald Dahl books by herself. While she loved hearing the Harry Potter book, Roald Dahl remains her favorite author, and *The BFG* (The Big Friendly Giant) remains her favorite book.

But *Harry Potter* isn't far behind.

I asked Claire, "Do you think *Harry Potter* is too scary for most little kids—say, under age eight?"

"No," Claire answered. "Seven or eight is okay. If they're five or under, I think it might be too scary." But Claire, like most of the seven-year-olds in her class, wasn't bothered by some of the spookier scenes.

"Do you think a lot of kids are reading the books before they're really ready—or do you think maybe the popularity of the series is inspiring kids to become better readers at younger ages, so that they can read the books on their own?"

Claire thought awhile about that one before answering. "I think if they can read it, they can understand it. Not everyone's reading it. Lots of kids have their parents read it to them. It helps if they read it to you because normally you might have trouble with a book like that. But when a grown-up is reading, they read it in a way that makes it easier for you to understand. And you can stop and ask questions if there's something you didn't get."

I asked Claire if she was worried that by the time she was ready to read the rest of the series on her own, Harry would be too old for her. He's 11 at the start of the first book but by the fourth book, he's already 14. "Do you think in future books, when Harry is 15 or 16, he will still be as interesting to younger kids? Or would you prefer to hear more about Ginny's adventures at Hogwarts, since she's closer to your own age?"

Claire responded, "No, not really. I like Ginny, but she isn't that interesting. But I might like it if Harry stayed the same age in a couple of the books."

My last question was "What was your favorite part?"

"I liked the ending."

Dear Harry Potter,

I've got a couple questions that I want to ask you:

What is it like to be famous?

What is your favorite class at Hogwarts?

What is the most boring class that you have to take?

What, in your opinion, is the bravest thing you've ever done?

After I heard your story, I began wishing that when I'm 11, I would get a letter asking me to come to Hogwarts and telling me that I'm a witch. That's what I'm wishing, even though all my relatives are Muggles. Well, if any of my relatives are witches or wizards, I certainly don't know about it.

Yours truly,
Emma
Age 10
Washington, D.C.

Dear Harry,

I really wish that I were you! It would be so cool to be able to do magic spells just like that-zap! Hogwarts seems to be a really good school; I'd really like to go there. Is Malfoy still annoying you? Don't worry about him. He's so stupid that he can't tell the difference between his own face and a pig's! (That is, if there *is* any difference!) I really hope that you and Hermione become head girl and boy in your seventh year.

Who's going to be the new captain of the Gryffindor Quidditch team? Wood left in your third year and in the year after that you had the Triwizard Tournament. It'll probably be you! By the way, would you know who's the new Defence against the Dark Arts teacher? The Defence against the Dark Arts teacher from a school over here just left to go to England. Maybe he'll be your new teacher. My friend told me about him. His name is Professor Hufe, and he's an aboriginal. (Pronunciation: *Hyoof*) He's really skinny. Every time you look at him you get this feeling that his bones are going to break any second. Hufe's an animagus, too; he turns into a kangaroo. He talks in a deep, growly voice that sort of scares you: Every time he talks to you, you feel like you're in trouble, even when he's come to give you a reward for working well.

If I was at your school, my favorite lesson would probably be Charms, and my favorite teacher would be Professor Flitwick. How's Ron? Maybe I could come to Hogwarts sometime and have a go on your Firebolt. There's a new broomstick in Australia-the model's called Lightning Crush. It's so fast that when it's moving it just looks like a silver blur. It has a sparkling silver handle with an orange lightning bolt on it. It has a tail of perfectly straight twigs, all helping it to go faster. The lightning bolt on it is like an accelerator. When you touch it, you go faster. When I get enough money I'm going to buy one for myself because I want to learn how to fly. You seem to absolutely love flying. I'll keep it in perfect condition and hide it in a secret cupboard for extra security so that if you visit sometime you could have a go on it. I'm a Muggle, but I have plenty of friends who are witches and wizards, so I know a lot about your world.

From,
Amy
Australia

To Harry Potter,

What's the funniest spell you've wanted to learn? I would love to turn myself invisible and spook out the teachers while they were in the lobby and scare them so they think it's a ghost. Everyone would be talking about it! Ever think of going into adoption? I would if I were you. Those relatives of yours are mean and nasty. I wish you could zzzzaaaaaapppppp them into frogs-but you're not allowed to use magic outside school grounds. Hey, what if you take them to Hogwarts and then zzzzaaaaaapppppp them into frogs, big, slimy ones!! Trick them somehow! I would do it, Harry!

"Warpeny, depeny, loopiny, soggies! Turn these Muggles into three slimey froggies!!"

Well, it was just an idea!!!

Say hello to everyone at Hogwarts for me,

From,
Edwina (Muggle)
Age 11
Worthing, West Sussex,
England

Dear Harry,

How is it at Hogwarts? Have you had anymore spectacular Quidditch wins? I hope Malfoy isn't bothering you too much. Has Professor Trelawney seen anymore death omens? Don't take them seriously. I know you can easily survive another attack from Voldemort. Oops! I mean You-Know-Who. Anyway, I hope to read about some more of your adventures soon. I think you are a lot like your father. I visited a Web site with a Hogwarts yearbook from when your parents were there. I didn't know your mother was in Slytherin with Snape, Lucuis Malfoy, and Tom. I think that might also be the reason why you can speak Parseltongue. Well, anyway, make sure Neville doesn't melt any more cauldrons in Potions and make sure Ron doesn't flatten Malfoy . . . Tell him to leave some for me, okay? I hope to talk to you again soon.

From,
Jess
Perth, Western Australia

P.S. Tell Hermione to give Malfoy another slap across the face from me.

P.P.S. Make sure Hermione doesn't tire herself out on schoolwork; she has to have some energy left to save you from the clutches of Voldemort.

Dear Harry,

I wish I could live at Hogwarts and have adventures like you. I am like Hermione, though my hair is not as bushy. If I were at Hogwarts, I would want to have a dog as my pet. Do you know Felina? She is a fairy that visits my room when I am asleep.

Good luck,
Lily
Age 8
Davis, Californi

Dear Harry,

I want to know if you can get me a spell book on all the magic spells at Diagon Alley. I love magic! It's one of my favorite things! I really want one. Hedwig can fly it over. I live on Main Street in Evanston, Illinois. I hope you can manage that. Also, I'm 8.

Love,
Matt
Evanston, Illinois

Dear Harry,

How are things going with your classes? I hope that Snape is taking it easier on you. Maybe someone should put a ban on evil teachers. You could say that you don't get a good education being taught by monsters. Do you think Dumbledore would fall for that? Somehow I don't think so!

How is your Quidditch practice going? I go for the Woolongong Warriors, they're an Aussie Quidditich team.

I have to go now, but maybe I'll send you an owl in the holidays!

From,
Helen
age 10
Melbourne, Australia

Dear Harry,

How's it going at Hogwarts? Are you still training regularly for Quidditch? I wish I had Quidditch at my school. It must be so fun to be able to ride on a broomstick. How old would Hedwig be? When you're older, do you want to become an Amnigus? If you would, what would you be? How are Sirius and Buckbeak doing? I hope that they are happy.

Sincerely,
James
Age 11
Perth, Australia

Dear Harry (if this is Harry Potter),

I hope you get this letter. My stupid owl, Ketchat, that I got yesterday, didn't understand the instructions I gave over and over. After all of that I threw him out the window with my letter. He could hardly fly!

I would have written a letter to you many years ago, when I first met you (oops, we've never met) but this is the first time I have been able to persuade my mom that wizards really exist. (People these days! They can't believe anything they haven't seen!)

Enough about me! What about your cool, exciting, adventurous life at Hogwarts? When do you think Lord Voldemort will finally figure out a way to kill you? (I think that hollow-headed stupid thing won't ever have enough brains, or any brains, to kill you!) Will Dudley ever lose a couple of pounds? (Never!) When will Ron's, Hermione's and your next adventure be? I have a feeling it's going to be really soon!

Sincerely,
Your new best friend,
Diane
Age 11
Winnetka, IL

P.S. Make sure Hedwig and Ketchat get along.

Dear Harry,

How are you? I am fine. Are you enjoying Hogwarts this year? Do you have an interesting Defense Against the Dark Arts teacher? How is Quidditch going?

You don't know me, do you? My name is Sarah. Don't worry about how I know about Hogwarts, because if you did know, you'd get extremely scared or, as Americans put it, freaked.

I was wondering if I could go to Hogwarts too. It sounds like an extremely cool school and I could do with some learning of witchcraft.

How are Hermione and Ron? Gotten into any fights lately? How are Fred and George? Blown anything up recently?

You don't get a chance to watch many Muggle movies or

read Muggle books, do you? Oh well, the school's library books will have to do. Try checking out "Where the Black Basilbush Grows" from the library. It's a classic but very sad. Or, at least suggest the book to Hermione.

Well, I just wanted you to know that I support every adventure that you have had, are having, and will have.

Again, don't worry about how I know about you, your school, your adventures, your sports, your friends (and future girlfriends?). It would just worry you. But I suppose getting a letter from someone unknown, who knows everything about you would worry you too. But you have to be used to getting weird things by mail now, right? I mean, the cloak, the Firebolt, the letter of acceptance into Hogwarts.

Anywho . . .

I hope that my owl, Athene, who is ancient, can make the trip to take this letter to you.

Please write back soon.

Yours,
Sarah

P.S. Sorry I haven't sent you any birthday gifts, but I don't think that Athene could have made the trip. I would have sent you plenty of stuff, though. Honest!

Interview with Sarah

My favorite characters are Fred and George because they're so funny, but smart at the same time. Very interesting. I'd love to know them. I believe I identify most with Hermione because she loves reading and I love reading. She studies continuously, which I don't, but still, she's as close to me as any of the characters get. Harry and I don't really have a lot in common. He's like me in that he likes competition and sports and dislikes Malfoy with a passion, but he's different from me in every other aspect.

I've always loved reading, but *Harry Potter* has gotten me into several different types of books, from *The Hobbit* and the rest of *The Lord of the Rings* to *The Death Gate Cycle*. It's neat noticing the similarities and differences between the stories.

I would love to be a witch! What magic would I like to do? Hmmm . . . the Summoning Spell (*Accio* homework!) and Charms. I would absolutely love to play Quidditch. I'd be a beater, though. And I would definitely go to Hogwarts or a sister school. Hogwarts is one of the coolest schools I've heard of.

I think it's sorta obvious that Harry's going to get a girlfriend, but I think it would be very cool if someone he horribly disliked was, in fact, a relative of his! Malfoy is his cousin or something like that. And, although Ms. Rowling keeps making insinuations that Harry is going to die, I would be very sad if that happened.

Why do I love Harry? He's funny, creative, gets on my nerves, can usually find an answer to any problem, can usually get himself INTO any problem, and he's as stubborn as a dwarf.

Harry Potter's fans are always kids at heart, even if they're past school age. . . .

Dear Harry,

I'm not a kid. In fact I'm nearly 23 years old, but I love hearing about your day-to-day life, full of fun and adventure. But also full of pain and sorrow. But you must realize, Harry, that it is importatnt for all of us that you keep standing you ground when Lord Voldermort is around.

You have the best of friends anyone could ask for. Ron and Hermione will always be there for you, and never forget that. Also, don't worry about what the Dursleys think: They are nothing compared to you. Harry Potter, stick around and let me join you in the fascinating world of Hogwarts School for Witchcraft and Wizardry.

I wish you the very best of luck in your fifth year at Hogwarts.

The friend you will never meet,
Luke
Age 22

P.S. I am from England so I hope this gets to you.